CW01572626

Chicane

Ronnie Price

Paperback ISBN 1-904312-098

Published in the UK by MX Publishing

GEMS, 5 Kings Head Parade, High Street, Wendover, Bucks HP22 6DX

Printed and bound by Antony Rowe Ltd, Eastbourne

'MOTOR SPORT IS DANGEROUS'

That's what the public notices say at racing circuits and it applies
not only to drivers but also to team owners and sponsors:
danger on the track and in the financial world.

The book is dedicated to all those who make motor sport happen,
giving me and millions of others so much enjoyment.

Acknowledgements

Thanks to my wife Sue who encouraged me. Also to Lucy who converted my scrawl into comprehensible text.

I finished the glass of champagne – not premier cru but quite drinkable – as the TAP airbus began its descent into Lisbon airport. The light changed suddenly as we banked in the early evening sunset. I like sunsets, I notice them, collect them or rather their memories.

I was feeling pretty good, elated even, the champagne helped but it was much more than that. I had just taken up a new appointment: roving Ambassador for British motorsport. The UK makes eighty percent of all the world's racing cars, rally cars and components worth one billion sterling a year in exports. Finally someone had woken up to the idea that Formula One was a perfect image for the new Britain. High tech., world leader and bags of style, glamour. It was something I had been pushing for quite a long time.

Now I had landed the job with joint funding from the motorsport industry, the government trade body and various UK teams. I had a nice three year contract: not a bad salary and some attractive perks one of which was to go as a VIP to all the F1 Grand Prix in some fairly exotic places.

This was why I was just landing at Lisbon to attend the Portuguese Grand Prix. I hadn't been to Portugal for a while but I remembered it is an elegant city with graceful avenues, but delicately faded like a beautiful woman with classic bone structure, ageing gracefully.

Like most airports it was in the process of being re-built but I followed the crowd and I was soon on the way to the taxi rank. I couldn't help noticing the woman in front, a couple of people between us. The walk first caught my attention. Some women walk like that, with a special lithe grace. A subtle female sway allied to an athlete's balance. As we got into the taxi queue I could see her more clearly. Not too tall, soft straight red hair. I tried to get a look at her legs but tripping over the guy in front's bag didn't help and made me look a wally. I flattered myself that she noticed the incident and smiled but I'm sure it was an illusion. Ah well. She disappeared a couple of taxis ahead of mine. Another of the many mysterious and beautiful women I shall never see again. What might have been…?

I checked in at the Tivoli Jardim just off the main drag - the

Avenida da Liberdade. Actually The Jardim is at the back of the Tivoli main hotel. It's smaller, cheaper and as I remember, nicer that the Tivoli proper. The pleasant smiling porter took the key, grabbed my case and ushered me into the waiting lift. We reached the top floor and the lift shuddered to a stop. We trundled along the corridor and he opened the door into a pleasant room. You never have any change for the porter do you? But he seemed happy with some English coins and showed me all the rooms mod. cons. – also a spectacular view over the city. Another dollop of sunset. I checked the time making a mental note to deduct a couple of minutes. My dear to the heart and purse, Rolex gains a minute a month and I hadn't adjusted it; but there is no way I would exchange its elegant stainless steel for a titanium microchip mini computer watch. Five thirty: there might still be someone at the Embassy. There was. The First Secretary Commercial – my main contact. James Ridley.

"Hello Jim. I just got here and I thought I'd check with you. Mind you I didn't think you diplomatic chaps worked much after lunchtime." He chuckled over the phone.

"Good old days – long since gone I'm afraid. Anyway it's nice to hear from you, Dan. Everything is going well so far but

I expect we shall have a few disasters later on."

Jim was one of the new breed of Embassy people. Down to earth – Midlands accent – pretty damned efficient. I'd had a lot of phone and fax contact with him before I'd come out and I liked dealing with him.

"Dan, I've got a final briefing seminar with the Ambassador tonight, otherwise I'd pick you up for a few jars and we could have dinner. But I don't know what time I'll be through with HE. Why don't you come to the Residence tomorrow, 10'ish, and we can have a look at the set-up and talk it through. I could suggest somewhere for dinner but based on our last get-together I expect you'd rather find some less than salubrious dive."

It was true that we had met one night in the West End where attractive young ladies were a major attraction. Just looking.

"OK, Jim, that's fine. I'd like to go over the programme early on to check the set-up and then maybe go out to the circuit. Have we got the press organised?"

"I think so. A few of them seem intrigued by the idea. So we'll probably get something."

We were talking about a reception to be held at the British

Ambassador' Residence – an elegant building in old Lisbon. There could be a number of F1 cars – empty chassis – displayed in the gardens. The whole thing could be floodlit – classy displays – a short speech by the British Minister of Sport and world champion Damien Miller. The Portuguese PM would be there and probably the President with all the local great and good. But no local Brits except local car importers. Rover were represented with the MGF starring and Jaguar were featuring the S-type and XK-8. Jim concluded his up-date for me and went off to brief the Ambassador.

While I was unpacking I worked out a scenario for the evening. I sometimes think I live in a fantasy world – which is why I'm not bad as a marketeer. My mind wandered over a Peter Cheyney scene. Thirties' style cocktail bar, high chromium bar stools, dramatic entrance of cool blonde with patrician looks, in a superb cut velvet dinner gown, a cleverly cut slit revealing a flash of beige silk stocking ...

The reality was often different. What's on cable TV in the hotel room; ring down for a club sandwich and half a bottle of fizz. No, I thought it's worth the effort to go down to the hotel bar, have a cocktail, live a little.

Modern lifts are all mirror and it's impossible not to regard your image, especially if the lift is empty. Medium to tall, fiftyish, thick grey hair, blue eyes and a sort of well-lived in English type of face. Nicely set off if I may say so by Polo blazer, button-down, slacks and the statutory J.P. Tod driving shoes.

The Tivoli Jardim bar is not retro-thirties but it does have bar stools. She wasn't blonde, she was red-haired. The dress was velvet with spaghetti string shoulder straps. There was no need for a slit in the skirt which was devastatingly short displaying most of her entrancing super-long legs. She was the girl I'd seen in the airport taxi queue. When I see a wonderful pair of legs I know I'm a leg man – until I see softly curving breasts, or a great bum. No, no, I'm definitely a leg man. I think. But enough of these sexist thoughts.

I perched on an adjacent stool – not the easiest bits of furniture to mount unless you're a trained athlete. I needed something to do while I thought out my strategy, but I resisted looking at the cocktail list – that's naff.

"Yes, Sir?", said the Portuguese barman, immaculate in his high-collar stewards' jacket. I think his eyes flicked very quickly from me to the lady and back.

"Let me buy you a drink", she said. Her voice was soft and

spicy with a light Irish accent. I know Irish accents. I lived there for a few happy years. I was gob-smacked. Is this happening to me, really? Come on. Not to me. I think not.

"Well, that really is extremely kind." I heard this clipped English Bondish voice, which had to be mine, say. "I'd love a dry Martini."

"How do you like it, sir?", asked the barman. "Our normal mix here is very dry."

"That sounds just about right." I smiled benignly at him, and at her.

I turned towards her. She looked wonderful. Before I could finish a full inventory she said,

"You were on the flight from London. You fell over your suitcase in the taxi rank. Something must have distracted you. You looked so funny and it made me laugh; so I thought it might be amusing to have a drink."

Three Martinis later and I was anybody's. Or at least hers. Our stories were out in a run of words, interruptions, false starts and explanations. She was the communications director for the O´Horan team – image, PR, supporter's club. Same business as me, really. I would have met her anyway in the course of the job. We were getting on nicely.

Then my heart sank; coming up to Kate – first name terms now – was an exceptionally attractive young man: a bit of a hunk in female parlance. Thick black hair, nicely tanned with your average super-star looks. Kate turned and slid off the stool gracefully showing a few more inches of thigh. Hold up stockings I think. The lacy top is the give-away.

"Hold-ups" said Kate reading my over-transparent mind. Then she took a couple of steps towards the new comer.

"Pedro, Pedro, it's so lovely to see you. Heh, you are looking good. How are you feeling?"

I recognised him now. He was an up-and-coming-young Portuguese driver. British Formula 3 series. But he had had a bad crash early in the season. I seemed to recall that he hadn't raced since then.

"Hello, Kathy, I'm so pleased to be with you again." He smiled, lovely teeth and kissed her on both cheeks. Polite, but… "I'm really much better now. I'm walking quite OK but I must do the physiotherapy each day. We have to wait to see."

His English accent was very good like most Portuguese but just a shade stilted, Kate, Kathy? turned to me.

"This is João Pedro Ramos; and this is Dan Piercy. We are

all in the motorsport business."

She explained what my new role was and he said politely that he thought it was a very important job. He had been racing in England and British motorsport was "tops".

Pedro told us that he would be out at the circuit next day because he was standing in as a commentator for RTP 1 television during practise and the race. He seemed to know Kate pretty well. Why did he call her Kathy? Apparently they had met during his season in the UK. He looked a bit young for her if you don't mind my saying. We all chuntered on – no more drinks though; he didn't. This was typical of many of the contemporary drivers: very professional; lots of training and health care. Not like some of the hell-raisers in the fifties.

Eventually it seemed that we would all have dinner together at the hotel which was nice but not entirely what had been in my mind. And he would pick Kathy up next morning and drive her to the circuit. He was doing a feature on O'Horan. Hmm. I was feeling side-lined. Suddenly this promising evening the result of startling serendipity, was oozing away. The head-waiter who recognised Pedro and also had an eye for Kate's super-mini, ushered us towards the dinning-room with an important strut and an oversized menu.

Then suddenly the game changed again. A small but beautifully formed Portuguese girl came towards us – almost running on her size three high heels.

"Oh, Oh. So sorry. It's terrible. I couldn't get a taxi."

When she got into range she promptly kissed Pedro on the lips. Then a quick cheek buss with Kate. Both Kate and Pedro were laughing.

"Cidália, my love, it is quite impossible for you ever to be on time. Never have I known it." Pedro with his arm round her shoulders introduced her to me.

"Cidália de Rosário, my beautiful but always late fiancée." The penny dropped. The name Rosário. He was the Chairman of the Portuguese bank which had sponsored Pedro in Britain. Well now, things were looking up. I entered the dinning-room with a youthful spring – or was it the built-in J P Tod factor?

It was a nice meal. Everyone talked a lot, mainly about motor racing. I possibly talked too much. I often do after a few glasses of wine. We drank a Portuguese Bairrada and it was good. It must have been almost midnight when we got into the lift to go upstairs. Kate's floor was one below me. There was a pleasant frisson in the atmosphere. Kate leaned back in the corner of the lift, one elegant leg folded nonchalantly over the other and a wicked smile curving her lips. The lift stopped. We both got out.

"Walk you to your room", I said lightly. Eyebrow raised. As we arrived at 304 she leaned over slightly to swipe the key card and the stretch of her body sent a tingling tremor – lust I suppose – into my nerve centre. She turned, opened the door wide and smiled.

"Good night, Dan."

Her kiss brushed my lips and she was gone.

Paris Thursday night

The wrought iron gates opened to let the dark windowed Mercedes 600 pass through with into the flag-stoned courtyard, quiet and cool under the Paris night sky. The house was one of those unobtrusive and quietly elegant buildings. The driver got out and after looking precisely around the courtyard area opened the back door to let out a small neat figure. In the light of the open door his Asian features could briefly be seen.

The driver walked with him to the entrance of the building, relaxed, professional and watchful. Once in the smaller man was led by a Filipino butler to a first floor room. Two of the men siting at the dark baize covered table were also Asian. The third man was not. They shook hands perfunctorily and the non Asian was introduced. When they were seated again he began to speak in English. They listened and watched impassively. At the end the lost arrival asked a few bullet point questions. How much? When? How soon for a result? What guarantees? He seemed satisfied with the answers, although he looked intent when getting to the point about guarantees. He nodded and looked around at the other Asians. It was clear who was in charge and the others quickly nodded their agreement. There was no food or drink and forty minutes after its arrival the Mercedes passed out through the ornate gates which closed behind it.

I turned the MGF into the entrance of the Estoril circuit. I had picked the car up from Rover Portugal after leaving the Embassy. Everything seemed to be in place and the guest list was very impressive. The first event in my new career was looking good. Jaguar were providing one of their new S-types as the track car and were main sponsors of this extra event in the motor racing calendar. Estoril has always been a favourite track with the drivers but had lost its place in the official F1 calendar because major improvements were needed to the circuit. Now it was making a comeback.

As I was parking it was great to hear the special sound of V10 racing engines – from growl to shriek – incredible controlled power. A very sexy sound which set the scene well. As ever I could feel the familiar thrill.

After a bit of pushing and shoving – and flashing my VIP paddock pass – the marshals let me through. Same the world over: they like to play tough. But to be fair there are so many potential gate-crashers that the officials have to be tough.

I threaded my way through the rather large crowd of hangers-on, the ratio is about five hundred to each racing car, I reckon. I wanted to check a few things with the teams and at the Johnson motor home I got hold of Ricky Bundell my team liaison contact. Each UK team had given me a contact. We sat down for a coffee.

"So how's it going?" I said as I sipped the strong black espresso. Ricky pulled a face.

"Tyres", he said. "The surface of this new track is very grippy and it looks as though tyres are going to be a real problem. The new sharper corners are tough too. You can't run too much down-force because you need maximum speed on the straight and we're sliding a lot."

The new regulations – grooved tyres and less efficient aero-dynamics – were designed to make things more difficult – to make the racing closer. In about an hour the cars would be going out for the official practise – the one which set the positions on the starting grid – and they had to get the tyres right. The compound chosen for practise had to be used in the race. Hand rubber compounds lasted longer – and might reduce the number of time-consuming pit-stops – but didn't have the high grip levels of soft rubber.

I went on to the Brezzona garage - technically an Italian team but a British designed car based at Silverstone with major UK technical input. It ways the same story on tyres - "Low-Wear" one of the F1 tyre suppliers, were going to have its work cut out to find the optimum compound. But anyway the Brezzona guys were in good form and they were good and ready for the British F1 party.

"That's if Mr Step-on-it doesn't put one of the cars into the tyre wall and we have to work all night on a re-build." said one of the more lugubrious mechanics.

As I strolled away I looked round. It was a bright and beautiful scene. The brilliant reds and blues – strong vibrant yellows - dotted round the paddock blended tastefully somehow with the beautiful people. Motor racing has always attracted them and they were certainly there. I spotted Count Padoli the Comendatore of Scuderia Fratelli looking Italian elegant in a discreet blazer and stylish sunglasses in contrast to the Scuderia Fratelli Italian red polo shirts of the team members and supporters – the 'travelling tifosi'.

I took a look round the O'Horan camp - I knew I'd saved it until last: I was hoping Kate might be there. Out of luck though. I looked at the Rolex. I had to meet a TV camera crew to do a short piece about how good Great Britain was in F1.

Then I saw him and he saw me. This was bad news. Sadly Ben Brentrock, the creator of modern Formula One had retired. My God, what that guy had achieved. He really was up there with just a handful of really top world businessmen. Modern Formula One enthusiasts owed him so much. But now a totally new company had been formed, Global F1 - Telesport, with total control of Formula One live programming and I certainly felt that the Brentrock touch was sadly missed. It needed his vision and ability to get creative but competitive people working together. The Chief Executive of this new money-spinner was one Gary Enders. He and I are not good friends. Now he was moving very definitely in my direction. He's a handsome guy, the bastard. Well over six feet, athlete's body and a face not unlike a series of James Bond look-alikes. As if that isn't enough rumour has that he has the biggest one in the paddock. If it is true one of the beneficiaries is my ex-wife who divorced me to marry him. Way back we had been buddies in Formula Ford and saloon car racing - shared an apartment near to Brands - but only a couple of years or so after I got married I discovered that he was screwing my relatively new wife. There was a helluva bust up. Even though we are part of the same world of motor racing we seldom speak now. Never if I can help it. We generally avoid one another. I certainly keep out of his way. He came up to me. Actually he was looking quite odd. Slightly vacant eyed, ropey complexion. A touch in fact unwell. Good. I did not look at him with the welcoming smile. Far from it, my eyes were a touch frosty, I'd say. He offered a hand, which I declined, and a tentative smile.

"I need to talk to you. Soon. Not here though." He spoke quietly, almost secretively. He even did a somewhat furtive look around to make sure that we were out of earshot of others in the paddock.

"Steady on" I said. "What is this all about? I didn't think we have too much to say to one another, Enders, ever." He seemed to lean forward to make his point.

"It is really, really important. Trust me."

Now that was an unlikely scenario – I could feel my eyebrows snapping in disbelief - but I was sort of intrigued. He put his hand on my arm and put his dark-brown lady-killer eyes close to my face.

"Please" he said. "Please." His voice was gritty with an edge of frenzy.

"OK" I said, pushing his hand away. "After the practise we can meet in Cascais. The Falcon Hotel. Say 3.30."

He nodded and muttered his thanks, displaying a totally foreign level of humility.

We went off in different directions. As I wound my way through the pit-lane throng, nodding here and there to various friends and contacts in different team colours, I pondered about Gary Enders and what he wanted.

About halfway through official practise Wolff Bros in the Brezzona was unexpectedly on pole. In the earlier races he had not really been on the pace but at Estoril the team seemed to have found a better set-up. I could see that in the Brezzona pit they were looking much more cheerful. Maybe a little more power from the engine or better torque. A good torque band makes a car so much more drivable. Or it could be some fine-tuning of the aerodynamics. That was proving to be crucial with the new tyres which give much less grip.

I went to watch from turn one. What I really wanted to see was a British driver in a British car up at the front. In fact going a stage further I hoped it could be Jonathan Piercy. He was a nephew, a protégé and something of a prodigy. He wasn't from the karting school where so many modern drivers got started. He had gone into Formula Ford at eighteen and had been outstanding. A top Formula 3 team spotted his talent and he went in as a test-driver. Terrific experience. Half way through the season one of the team drivers injured himself and Jonathan took his place. He won every one of the remaining races. Incredible. He vaulted up into Formula One as number three in the Johnson Racing team. This year cars were allowed to have three drivers and he was proving to be very quick, but also neat and stylish. Many people have compared him with the young Stirling Moss – and no higher praise is possible, in my book.

I watched as a Scuderia Fratelli came into the corner a shade off line and onto a dirty patch; in a flash the car over-steered and the driver Guido Firelonni - was correcting a wicked slide. A few delicate wheel flicks and he accelerated out of the corner but that had certainly lost time on one of his fast laps. These days the times are so close and one hundredth of a second can cost you a grid place. There was no restriction on the number of practise runs a driver could have but there was a limit on the maximum number of tyres available, including the race.

An O'Horan in its distinctive canary and green livery came round going well and the engine sounding clean, picking up well on the way out of the corner. Slow in, fast out we used to say. But now it was brake late and hard, let the speed carry you deep into the corner and then power down for the exit. Then I saw a Johnson Racing appear and dive into the corner. It was Jonathan and he was steaming. Beautiful line. I could visualise his hands and feet at work. Left foot braking is the norm now so he would be stamping on the left pedal very hard, flicking the clutch-less gear shift on the squared off steering wheel, then as the car cleared the apex, getting quickly but smoothly on the gas. I was really pleased to seeing him going so well.

The next car though appeared to be handling like a pig; excessive under-steer as he turned into the corner so that the car ran wide; and vicious over-steers on exit. The driver - a promising young Brazilian - did well to keep it out of the gravel trap.

I wandered off down to a long straight to enjoy the rich blend of explosive sound and brazen colour as the cars ripped past at almost two hundred miles an hour.

The session was coming to an end and I made my way back to the pit area. I dropped in again at the O'Horan pit where the Boss was in good humour telling the tale to a guy from a leading magazine. It was obviously a good one by the grin which gradually cracked his face. I prowled around after waving cheerily to him, still looking for Kate. However still no luck.

The practise had ended and the grid positions were settled. Metzer in the O'Horan was on pole - no wonder the guvnor was in great form - and terrific news Jonathan Piercy was in the second spot.

I meandered across to the Johnson garage; I could see Jonathan chatting to the engineer looking at some print-outs from the monitor. I hung around until they had finished, looking around the garage area and swapping smiles and glances with a few of the guys and girls. A couple of female technicians now in this high-tech business. Probably a serious woman driver in a top team before too long.

Jonathan saw me and came over. As ever he had a nice warm smile. Twenty one years old, medium height, almost schoolboy demeanour, he was everyone's idea of a nice guy. He was very good-looking in a somewhat patrician way; and he was in very good physical shape. Hard training had honed a natural sportsman's physique. A good lad.

"Jonathan, pretty good. eh? You must be very pleased."

"Hi Dan," he said warmly. "Yes, I am feeling pretty good. The car is really going well, handles a treat. The set-up is perfect"

Set-up was one of his real strengths. Right from his days as test-driver he seemed to know what was necessary to improve the handling. Almost mystical really. But it meant that his race engineer could rapidly interpret the changes needed and Jonathan could start to attack the times.

"Dan, how's the new job going?" he asked. I told him.

"I'm still over the moon about, it - can't really believe it. Just the perfect job."

"Not for me", said Jonathan. "I'm really the lucky one. A racing driver with the Johnson team. Bloody Hell."

I'd known him since he had been at school. I'd seen him develop. He still seemed too young to swear. A late developer. Nothing outstanding in the academic stakes, not much good at the statutory ball games though he had become a useful scrum–half as he got older. It's amazing the part good luck plays in our lives, careers. He had drifted into a junior car salesman's job with a big Jaguar dealer and he had had the chance to do a run in a Formula Ford car at the Jim Russell school when the dealer organised a track day for clients. The school was impressed and after further trials agreed to run him with sponsorship from the Jag. dealer in a forthcoming series.

So, luck as ever played a key role. But he had the talent to ride it. It was going to be frenetic from now on without much chance to meet up so we left it a bit vague and agreed that if there wasn't a chance in Estoril we would meet for lunch in London. People were beginning to leave the paddock and the circuit. On my way to the car park I peeked again into the O'Horans pit , but no Kate. Daft really, but she had somehow got to me. Ah well, dream on.

Chapter 3

Despite the time of year, early Spring, Cascais portrayed a pleasant holiday atmosphere. Pretty well all the bars and cafés in the waterfront area were open and a lot of folk, tourists and locals, seemed to be enjoying a late afternoon drink or "bica" of coffee at the outside tables. The air felt good: soft and clean and stimulating. The low slung sun was flickering over the light movement of the water. It was going to be a splendid sunset.

My mood had picked up. I was not looking forward to my meeting with Gary but I could now go into it in a more positive frame of mind. The truth is that he does make me feel threatened, a bit second rate. Not too difficult really to understand why, though, when you reflect on our relationship.

When we were racing together, in juniors and in saloons, he had always been quicker and had attracted the attention of the press and better teams. He had done brilliantly at Cambridge in engineering and was in the running for a cricket blue. I have to admit that he was a first-class batsman.

Somehow in those days I had never got my act together, and always felt that I was standing in the shadow of his limelight. I mean it was nothing too obvious: I don't think other people noticed. But I felt it subconsciously. I think that was why when I met Gabriella, and she seemed to prefer me, it was so important.

We had stayed close friends even though he had moved quickly up the success ladder, first in property, then finance and eventually into serious motorsport management. Neither of us really had the talent to go the top as drivers and our Formula Ford days had been largely sporting - although naturally, he did go one up on me by getting a trial with a Formula 3 team. Then we were into the tin-tops, saloons but it never went anywhere.

The big break-up came when he seduced my wife Gabriella just a couple of years after we were married, and she left me. Although I have never really been sure that she had not seduced him. Before and after the marriage we had spent a lot of time together socially - a foursome really with his live-in girlfriend Jessica. A nice girl I thought - ex-deb, ex-model, and in due course extra to his requirements. I should have picked up a message when he gave her the push and we became a threesome. But I was still in the dreamland belief that Gabriella really loved me; and Gary brought along the odd, different girl to dinner from time to time I thought it was just that he was between partners. He'd had a long string of women since I had known him. Reluctantly you have to accept that he is attractive, sexy I suppose although it is always difficult for a man to judge what attracts women.

In the end it was the classic in-flagrant scene. There was a meeting in Edinburgh which I had to attend and I was staying the night up there. But at Heathrow I didn't feel too well - there was a rotten dose of "flu" about - so I cancelled the trip and decided to return home. I tried to call home but as usual my mobile had run down and I had no coins or BT card. Anyway I didn't think it was important and I was feeling too groggy to care. So I got the car from the long-term and hit the road. As I turned into the small mews where Gabriella and I had set up home, l saw the gunmetal blue Porsche outside the house. I stopped. Suddenly a cold hard hand squeezed my heart. In that soul-searing millisecond I knew. A lot of things suddenly jigsawed into place. I waited a few minutes to clear my mind and control the sudden flush of bile. To think logically what did I want to do? What would the result be? What did I want to happen? Above all, though, I knew that I must know for certain.

Quietly, but with my heart banging like a heavy metal band drum, I went to the steps. Because it is a mews house the main rooms are at the top and it is difficult to hear noises in the entrance hall. I opened the door with some care. There was just the Banham lock - all that was needed when you have an alarm system. Inside I stood quite still and listened. I took off my shoes and went quietly up the stairs. I felt as slimy as hell but I had to do it. I expected to hear noises and I did. They were familiar. I stood almost petrified, unbelieving. But the noises grew louder, sharper and were joined by a male guttural barking sound.

In a trance I moved to the open door and saw them. She had her head back, eyes tightly closed, her mouth open with the gasping. He was on top and driving hard. At that moment they came together, spectacularly. That picture with my wife's legs clenching round his shoulders is engraved forever in my mind.

After that it was a tawdry French farce. They rolled apart realising I was there; shock horror, shouting and screaming. He stood there with his big thing still sticking out, no condom I noticed and I bashed him with my shoe. Eventually he left. I was ice numb. Then I came back to some normality. My wife and I talked. I knew I loved and wanted her. I thought we could get over this. OK it was a sexual fling but our marriage and life together was more important. Until it became clear that there was more to it. It had been going on for some time. She was deeply in love with him. She wanted a divorce. She was gone.

And that's what happened. From a pecuniary point of view I was lucky that because Gary was even then almost a millionaire, she did not want anything from me in the settlement - just a few personal things. So we split up with a fair amount of acrimony; and they lived happily ever after.

All of this stuff came flooding into my mind as I approached the attractive Falcon hotel in a side street by the side of the sea. I think my first dinner in Lisbon was on the balcony terrace of the Falcon looking out over the refreshing vista of Lisbon bay and the Tagus estuary.

There is a small discreet cocktail lounge and he was already in there. I went straight to the bar and bought a gin and tonic, then paid for it. I wasn't accepting drinks from Gary.

I sat down in the corner of his table.

"Well?" I said, voice like slate grey basalt. "I am in the deep shit," he said "and you are the only one who can help me."

"Ha." I could hear the calculated irony in my voice. "You have of course come to just the right man for help. Why the bloody hell do you suppose that I would have the slightest interest in helping you? I couldn't give a rat's fart about your problems." Anger and stress tend to enhance my verbal style. He looked at me, a trifle too cool and collected, I thought.

"You'll help me because you are a nice guy and because you are one of those people with a soft-heart. You can't help yourself. You can always be manipulated - no matter what. And secondly because of Gabriella. You've always stayed in love with her. She knows it, I know it, and you know it. Things between her and me are not so good; maybe she would come back to you."

Mixed emotions bounced around in my mind. Incongruously I felt a tingle in my groin at the mention of her name and the possibilities. Trouble is he was right. Although I may rant and rave and declaim famously my total hatred and contempt, I knew that in a push-to-shove situation I could well be shoved. The fact that I was sitting here at all said it all and he knew that.

"Go on." My voice indicated that I was prepared to listen.

"This is pretty unbelievable" said Gary. You can say that again a couple of times I thought as he went on.

"You know a fair bit about F1 and the industry. Well there are some dirty games being played out there - always have been; it's a mega billion bucks business, and I get my share. But this is much bigger, global stuff. You've got to keep it absolutely confidential. If for nothing else national interest. Although that's a bit fanciful at this stage. It's a major power struggle for the dominance of the auto business world wide. There is a well organised group of Asian power players which is positioning itself to control that business, not Japanese. They are outside the consortium. The big boys involved come from developing Asian countries... business lubricates you know. The strategy is simple. In future car sales will be all about brands like designer clothing. Technology is pretty standard. Difficult for anyone to win a lead let alone keep it, and the dough involved in development is becoming astronomical. The eco-groups are putting more and more pressure on the use of the car as a piece of convenience equipment. It is becoming much more leisure orientated. So the key will be to establish the brand names which people want to buy, cars which make them feel good to be seen in. Nothing new in this - there have always been prestige marques. But this is using the imagery to take over mass markets. The Far Eastern consortium realises that the key is Formula One. With its Universal TV/Satellite reach it can get to the hearts, minds and cheque books of 90% of the world population. There could be some big media moguls also interested in some way, but let's skip that for now."

He was beginning to interest me in this Boys Own Paper, yellow peril, dire warning. Lots of real-life stories and events knock the eye-teeth out of fiction.

"Now as you know I've been pretty successful in building up the FI business scene. Since Ben opted out, I've been making the running and one way or another pull most of the strings. Where the races are to be held, which TV companies get the rights, which teams are accepted, how the whole bloody thing comes together. Forget the officials, of course they do a vital job of looking after the admin. Their technical committees are theoretically responsible for the rules. But in the end they just write the specs. to implement rules which I think will make the racing action more attractive to the TV punters - and the advertisers. So, when the Asians want to get things done, who do they come to? Me."

The plot thickened as they say, and I began to get some idea of where we might be heading. I said nothing but raised my left-brow courtesy of Roger Moore. Just takes practise.

"The fact is they have got me by the balls, one at a time and a handful of pubic hair as well. When I took over Formula One I had to engage in some irregularities. Pay offs, secret funding even, and I am not proud of it - a bit of blackmail and coercion. I used indirectly, some semi Mafia contacts I knew in Naples. A couple of people died, but I knew nothing about that at the time. I would never have countenanced murder, ever. Or even physical harm. I just wanted a few people to be encouraged to go along with me. You've got to believe that. I know you think that I'm an unprincipled bastard. OK, but not a murderer."

He took a long slug of scotch - sucked it down. He was definitely struggling a bit to maintain the persuasive charm. I wasn't surprised. He swallowed, sighed a couple of times and pushed on. Nowhere else to go.

"They want me to move things around to suit their strategy. Oh it will start gently, kick out some of the existing teams. Not difficult. Push up the financial ante - the entrance fee. Create some performance requirements, ban some sponsorships. If the F1 unity arrangement had ever gone through with real teeth it could have been a problem, but ultimately self interest prevails. As things are we could easily force three teams out of Formula One. This gives the chance to put in three Asian brands. They would be uni-cars - the name on the engine would be the same as the car. No tobacco sponsors, just a couple of motor component or oil logos, brands which they own anyway. But the big names, aggressively displayed, would be their retail car brands. And of course they would do a total merchandising link-up with advertising, dealer promotions in main markets."

Gary grimaced un-charmingly. "It would go on from there. The TV coverage would be doctored, slanted to focus on them. They wouldn't expect to be doing any serious winning at first. But the presentation, the team gear would look stunning and with the right bias on the TV box they would gradually build up their message. Of course they want to attract the star drivers, the big names and they have the resources to pay for them. But they know that I can be pretty influential in who drives where. It gets worse." He turned and looked out over the pink-blue sea. I knew I was right about the sunset which was incredible as it silhouetted the Tower of Belém. But I didn't think he could see the Tower or the majesty of the setting sun. I knew he had no soul. You could see that his mind was 20.000 miles away somewhere in South East Asia. He turned and looked at me. I think it was intended to be a deep, convincing, manly eye to eye looking rather than just a look. I have to say it did not work for me.

"They are demanding that I start playing around with the rules, the regulations and the way they are implemented. They want to be not just winners but crushing winners. All the leading teams are so badly beaten that they lose sponsors, run out of cash, are forced out of the Formula scene or they are Aunt Sallies to highlight the Asian success. I think there is also the plan to scoop up some of the top names. I know that it sounds far-fetched but believe me these people are playing for enormous stakes; they are completely ruthless and they have unlimited resources." He stopped talking to take another drink.

"OK, it's not a pretty picture. Sounds like a Grimm's fairy story; but why tell me? Hell, in my new job shouldn't I be trotting off to tell the tale to someone in authority?"

He shrugged. "Who?" "What?" "What could they do?"

Somehow he was irritating the hell out of me. I tapped my finger on the table to emphasise my words.

"Well the police and fraud squad might have a passing interest in your own involvement." I knew it didn't sound convincing.

"There's no evidence other than that which they - the Asians have. Unless you have got a concealed mike." Now there was a thought... but too late to be useful.

This time we did lock our eyes and our thoughts.

"There's more isn't there?" My question sounded rhetorical. Gary didn't deny it.

"I'm already in. I have been setting up a few things for them. I'm implicated. I thought it wasn't much at first. Not too demanding. Not really hurting anyone - anyone who didn't deserve to be hurt. I suppose it was the easy way. It wasn't really the money."

Jesus, my mind jumped. As well as everything else he had also been taking money from the Asian gang. They had him over a barrel.

When he spoke again he acknowledge this.

"Now the pressure is on me. Of course it is blackmail. But who the hell cares? It's not like going to the police because you are being blackmailed about an affair. I am too much involved. It would finish me off in the racing game. Plus I´d probably go to jail."

This was not a good analogy as far as I was concerned. The word affair did not sit lightly on my over sensitive persona. I sensed we were coming to the crunch. With a despairing flick of the hand he continued in a dead-note voice.

"I've told them that I can't do any more, can't go any further. I'm in too deep already. It's too dangerous and too difficult. I want out. But they will not buy that. They could destroy me with the stuff they have got on my past dealing and what I've done for them - they pay-off. But that would blow the game. So we are now getting into the heavy threat scene. I know what they are capable of and it scares the shit out of me."

He looked up at me. "The threats include Gabriella."

I could see him running his tongue over his dry lips. It didn't look as though it would help much. "I don't know what to do." He said simply.

I reckoned that was the truth but I also had a nasty suspicion that he might be harbouring thoughts of a solution, temporary or permanent which might well involve this erstwhile cuckold – good old soft hearted, stupid, me.

"Where does Gabriella come into it?" I asked him cautiously, but I was sure he had spotted my underlying concern.

"They are proposing to take her hostage. We are just completing the regulations for the next five years and I have to make sure that the committees, constructors, organisers approve a new formula and new financial arrangements which will force out the smaller teams and let in the Asians. When that is signed and sealed - six weeks? She will be returned. Otherwise... Of course there is no way I can tell the police - which police? - and it will be planned on the basis that she is taking a long holiday overseas to see some old friends. It does hold water because we have been spending more and more time apart. I have told them that we are virtually separated and will be getting a divorce. Actually it's true, but they don't believe me. So as far as I know they will go ahead unless I can come up with something to stop them. That's why I want you to take Gabriella with you on your trips with the F1 circus." He slipped it out quite neatly, catching me off-balance. I stared at him in amazement.

"How the hell would that work? Gabriella might just have

something to say about it. And what about me? Just starting a new ruddy job! It's crazy. And why would your Asian chums accept it?"

"We'd have to explain some of it to her. The threats - and I've already told you I think she might not be dead against the possibility of you two getting it on again. And to the Asians it could be credible. It would make them stop to think. Oh I know it doesn't solve anything long term but it could put the lid on a bit of it. I mean, I'm really frightened for Gabriella. OK, it's over between us. It was only really ever a case of white hot sex. To be unusually honest I've met someone else very special. But I'm still worried to death about Gabriella."

He knew I was hooked. We chewed it over for a while. I was still totally hostile to him but eventually I agreed to have dinner with them back in London early in the following week. He promised to prepare Gabriella in advance. I almost believed him. One thing I knew for sure: I didn't know what I was getting into. Although I knew why. Unhappily.

He left the hotel first. I watched until that wonderful blood orange orb had quietly melted into the wine red sea. Or was I taking advantage of Homer.

I walked back to the car in pensive and somewhat

troubled mood. I got in and drove fairly slowly on the "*Marginal*" back to Lisbon.

There was an envelope pushed under my hotel room door, signed Kate. 'Sorry I didn't see you today at the circuit. Thought we might have had dinner tonight. I fly back early tomorrow. Maybe we will meet in London or Silverstone?'

London felt good in the early morning Spring air. A freshness which you don't find in naturally warm climates. It looked good too; spruced up after the Winter drabness.

I drove straight to my new office in Knightsbridge with handy underground car park. We had a small suite in a modern block backing onto the park, with a great view of the Household Cavalry doing their morning exercise rides.

My P.A. and general factotum Carolyn looked up as I went in and we exchanged pleasantries. She is dark, slim, and attractive but our relationship - so far anyway - was one of good friends and colleagues. Anyway she is married, happily I would surmise.

A pile of faxes - a neat pile - awaited me; another one of letters by the side and one unopened envelope marked 'personal/private' slap in the middle of the desk. Very good quality envelope and the light smell of a perfume which I thought I might recognise. How does that work? Do women dab it on the envelope along with a dab behind the ear? Sometimes, I suspect, a dab in the knickers, too.

I wondered with warm anticipation whether it could be from Kate. I had faxed my home & office contact details to her care of the O'Horan headquarters. I opened the envelope carefully and leaned back in my new leather executive chair to read it. It wasn't from Kate.

15 Cheyney Walk
London SWI
0171 229 7744

Wed, April 28th

Dear Dan,

I must talk to you. It is very important. I know how you feel but please talk to me. I'll be in touch.

Yours,

Gabriella

I looked unseeing across the park. Well now this is interesting, I thought. Just what is going on? Gary had said that he would be arranging the dinner with Gabriella to talk about the situation, but this had been written before he and I had talked in Cascais. OK let's first see how things go.

I put it out of my mind and attacked the paper. Some useful things were beginning to develop. The Prince was coming out to Monaco to host a celebrity party for the UK constructors. Former top British racing drivers were going to do a demonstration run in a Jaguar XK 8 at Spa just before the start of the Belgian Grand Prix. I was also working on something really special for Silverstone. One new thing caught my interest. There were plans for a special event in Ireland - at Dublin's Phoenix Park. It seems that the new President of Ireland was behind the idea and O'Horan team was much involved. They wanted to talk to me as a start to getting backing from some of the teams.

It was quite late when I left. Carolyn had already gone. Not a lot of point in rushing home so I parked off the square and walked round to a Café Uno. I found a table and ordered some good basic nosh - garlic sausages, a pile of mashed potatoes and a half bottle of Mouton Cadet; well, I was driving you see.

I felt curiously sad and lonely; ludicrous really with all the people I knew and the lively social life I enjoyed. But seeing a few young couples looking at each other as if they really were in love made me drift back in time - the worst kind of over-indulgence in mushy peas nostalgia. Won't do. Daft. The fact that these couples were probably extra-marital affairs or sex-driven one night stands also brought me back to the reality of men's and women's simple lust. On that ponderous note I tendered my Platinum Plus card, paid up and sauntered out, jacket slung sleeves-out on my shoulders.. No one noticed me going. London is that sort of place. Millions of people each one entirely enclosed in a personal oyster of life: money, health, job, love and fear.

Perversely I was still living in the mews where Gabriella and I had first set-up home and where I had first found out about her affair with Gary. Well, I reasoned, it is a very nice house in an extremely attractive and convenient setting. So what's the point of letting an emotional blow-up spoil it? Time would wash away the sharpest stabs of memory. It was always the sort of place I had wanted and I decided to hang onto it. Some consolation. I expect there was also some sentimentality.

A bonus was the drive-in garage and electric door. I went up the short stairway from the garage into the entry hall. A nice door finish in Cambridge blue. I switched on the light and dumped my case. I looked around: something was not quite right, I felt the prickling of hairs between my shoulder blades. I moved carefully but with a bit of bravado up the spiral staircase to the sitting room. I'd been here before – although in a different scenario I admit.

She was sitting in the twilight, eased back into my Charles Eames chair, legs elegantly stretching along the matching footstool. She looked at me quizzically but directly.

"What the hell?" I shook my head briskly as though to clear it.

"Gabriella. How did you get in? Why are you here?"

She looked at me with that powerful mix of feminine guile: a touch of direct challenge and gentle apprehension.

"I kept the keys - perhaps I thought that one day I might come back." She spoke clearly in a matter-of-fact Wedgwood voice - but beneath the cool laid-back tone I detected an edge of uncertainty; anticipation of a bruising reaction.

She seemed to have a catch in her voice as she went on.

"I sent you a note. I was going to get in touch but things have become serious rather more quickly than I'd expected. I'm so nervous, Dan."

I sat down and looked at her while I digested this. She leaned towards me.

"I know what Gary has told you about the Far East consortiums I think most of it's true. But I know he's becoming more and more involved and I am really frightened. He's been getting some long distance calls which are really getting to him. The last one this afternoon got him in a lather and he blurted out that they were threatening to kidnap me as a hostage. Then he tried to joke about it. I didn't find it at all funny. I've met some of the people he's been dealing with and they scare me."

Her large soft grey eyes found mine reflecting a hint of pleading and a touch of something else. These same lustrous eyes could be lethal to any male at up to three metres range, and on full beam might well blow up a Centurion tank. I could already feel my stern resolve shrivelling under their focused fire.

"So I just had somehow to get away. Out of the way. Not to be a problem to Gary; give him the chance to sort it out without having to worry about me. Not that he'd be too worried the way things are now between us."

She gave me both barrels with the grey eye routine. It might be working. In fact I was pretty sure it was. I looked away and pulled my mind back into line, a swift jerk back to reality.

"So what have you got in mind - where are you planning to hide-out if that's the word?" She didn't answer right away, masterly timing. "I thought perhaps I could stay here for a couple of days until I can sort something out. I haven't had a chance to think it through yet. It has all happened so fast."

I sighed and raised my eyebrows. "Gabriella, you know that's not a good idea. OK you have had a scare but I think you've over-reacting. Look this is London not Naples and this so called Far Eastern consortium is made up of serious business men who can't afford international scandal. They are not the Mafia, you know; and staying here sure as hell would not improve your situation with Gary, would it?"

"Gary is away - he's gone to a meeting in Paris, something about the threat to tobacco advertising. He told me just to behave normally but to make sure that the alarm was on and everything properly bolted and barred. And he said he was arranging for a security company to keep an eye on things. But I am just terrified now of being there alone. Look, let me just stay here until Gary is back; then we can all get together and see what can be done. We're hoping you can help."

Great I thought. I didn't need this. I've a great new job. I do not wish to become involved with some scandal in the Formula One world involving my ex-wife and the guy who pinched her from me.

She could see me wavering. She pressed home the advantage.

"I can stay in the spare room. I suppose it's the same."

Indeed it was. Just how she had designed and decorated it. I was bemused. All my gut feeling say 'no way, José'. But I am a softie: it was getting late and I wasn't too happy about her going back to the empty house at that time. Capitulation in the guise of compromise. Neville Chamberlain comes to mind. I waved my bit of paper. So appeasement isn't weakness is it? It's buying valuable time to prepare for war.

"OK, just for tonight, because it's so late. Tomorrow we'll sort something else out."

She exhaled – light string of air – and just said " Thank you". She relaxed stretching her long legs even further on the

Eames. I fixed a couple of scotches, a bit stronger than my usual night-cap. I sat uncomfortably as we sipped them. I looked at the watch. Just after 10.30.

"It's getting late." I said. "Been a long day for me and you must be whacked. Did you bring any night things with you?" She shook her head.

"I came out in such a rush once I decided."

"OK" I said, "let's see what I can find."

I went into my bedroom, then the bathroom and rummaged around.

"One shirt, slightly worn at the cuffs; long enough for you I'd say. And a new toothbrush. Oh, and this old robe". She smiled.

"Thanks."

Picking up these items she moved, graceful as ever, into the bathroom.

I poured another scotch and ruminated somewhat gloomily about life and a series of problems which seemed to be looming. Just a few days ago I had been full of enthusiasm. The new job – an upward gear shift in my life style. All seemed positive and good. Now some serious cracks were appearing.

The door buzzer cut through my reverie its jagged sound

snapping me back to the uncomfortable present.

I pondered for a sec, then flicked my eyebrows resignedly – it had become a mannerism - and put down the glass. When I opened the door my heart rocketed up; then just as quickly disappeared into my boots. Before I could do anything, Kate wearing a soft smile and a Dolce & Gabbana sling coat slid round me into the hall.

Thinking slowly I tried to intercept her but before you could say 'nice scent' she was half way up the stairs. I followed slowly, mesmerised by the even pace of her steps and the ever present swirl of thigh. The other lobe of my brain was pounding away ineffectually: what the hell to do?

She went straight to the Eames chair and composed herself comfortably on it. That lucky old chair was accommodating more than its share of lissom female bum this night.

"Do you have any Irish?"

Her first words were in that peaty voice and with a mischievous and highly provocative smile. She could see that I was ban-jaxed, tongue-tied - which she thought amusing - but she didn't know why. That little denouement was still to come. I still hadn't said a word and frankly nothing useful to say came to mind. So I went to get the Irish whiskey neatly removing

Gabriella's half-full glass en route. I brought a glass over to Kate. She looked incredibly beautiful her hair and eyes glowing in the rich soft light. Then I started to get my act together.

"Kate", I said. "just how did you get here? How did you find me? I mean it's great but..." She gave me a cool look with a soft warm centre.

"Well now that's a fine welcome. Sure this lovely fella seems to have forgotten that he faxed me his address, which I took to be something of an invitation". She was right. Now I remembered doing just that.

"Yes, but Kate..." I started to say. I got no further. She reached up and put a manicured finger nail on my lips. It tasted good. Again the soft Irish voice.

"Ah now, I think we have a little unfinished business, you and I love." Suddenly she slipped her hands round my neck and pulled my head down to her. Her kiss shimmered with promise. All my senses buzzed and hummed. I'd lost it.

Keeping her eyes fixed on mine she swung up easily from the leering Eames and slipping her arm through mine moved purposefully towards the bedroom.

"Kate ..." Again her finger on my mouth. I gave up. I

focused on the shapely sensitive finger and exquisitely manicured nail. I was on a free-fall to disaster. I may as well enjoy it while I could. I stepped back out of my mind and as a dispassionate observer watched it all happen. Before Kate could open the door it swung open itself and through it treading daintily came Gabriella. She looked great in the old Jermyn Street shirt. Turnbull & Asser, of course. The look was not compromised by the fact that the plimsoll line seemed to be a fraction above the pubic area.

This was impasse epitomised. These two beautiful creatures locked eyes with feminine ferocity. Neither said a word. Kate put me down-well, she let go of my arm - and I backed into the sitting room. I found my drink and sat down on the Eames. It was about time it was seriously sat upon. I waited for some action.

It seemed that the tableau was frozen in time but it can't have been more than a few seconds.

Suddenly Kate pivoted on her Kurt Geigers and walked straight out of the room and down the stairs. By the time I got to the top of the stairs I saw the front door click behind her. I opened it swiftly just as she was shutting her car door. She saw me and the window slid smoothly down. She appeared to be smiling again although I wasn't sure that there was any warmth or humour there. When she spoke however, the characteristic lilt was back.

"It seems we are ill-starred lovers, darling. I chose a bad time now, but there'll be another." Then with a blown-kiss and wave she was gone, leaving just the sound of hard acceleration re-bounding from the close walls of the quiet mews.

I walked somewhat wearily back into the sitting room. By now Gabriella had re-possessed the Eames.

"I'm sorry", she said.

I wasn't convinced that she meant it. Women are perverse and although she had dumped me I think she still felt she retained some proprietory rights. I shrugged philosophically.

"That was 'Kate O'Malley' the new PR Director at O'Horan the team sponsored by an Irish pop group. We met in Portugal and it could have been a beautiful friendship but that's buggered it, I reckon. Do you think she knew who you are?"

"Oh yes. If she's in Formula One, she'd know the wife of the boss." Gabriella said confidently. "Has she been here before, she seemed to know her away around"?

I didn't much want to talk about it. I had been building up

some nice thoughts about Kate. I just had the feeling that there was something there. Now it looked as if it was shot.

"No" I said. "But I had given her the address and she's the kind of woman who doesn't wait for a formal invitation".

I went over to the spare room and put on the light.

"Gabby, I think I'm going to turn in now, I've had it. The bed is made up. Extra blankets in the chest. Bottled water in the fridge. I'll see you tomorrow morning. No rush - it's Saturday. Then we'll have to think what to do. Good night."

I turned off the lights, grabbed a bottle of Malvern water and went to bed. I had thought it would be difficult to get off to sleep, but no.

I must have been in a pretty deep sleep because the next thing I became aware of was a smooth soft finger gently stroking my erect penis. The erect penis was fairly normal most nights. The stroking finger was not.

I turned sharply to find Gabriella in bed at my side. I shook my head to clear the sleep and glared at her.

"I think by being here tonight I deprived you of your... sexual release. I'd like to make it up to you." As she spoke she stopped stroking and loosely clasped her hand around it.

"Gabriella, we finished long ago. There's no point in going

back. It's crazy. I don't want to. The memory is too hard. It would be a mess." But the movement of her hand was making talk difficult.

"Dan, this isn't just for you. I want it too. I'm so tense. Being scared does that and I haven't had it for quite a while. It's just now, tonight; a couple of people who need some emotional outlet."

There was no way I could resist. Her caress was subtle but insistent. I turned towards her, threw back the sheets and began stroking her back. Long slow firm strokes finishing on the mound of her buttocks. The way I knew she liked it.

The next hour was a kaleidoscope of images, sounds, and re-called pleasures. The unique sensation of drawing the back of the hand over crisp pubic hairs. Her extraordinary athleticism when she hooked her feet so high around my back. The glorious moment when the first thrust went right up. Her divine gift of muscular control to give exquisite satisfaction.

Afterwards I felt exultant at having had this woman again - after she had rejected me. I also felt terrible: guilty and despising myself for so easily being seduced - and without a condom ... This time I didn't fall asleep as quickly. When I was woken by light through the part-drawn curtain I was the only one in bed.

Chapter *5*

I got out of the bed thoughtfully. I didn't think that Gabriella would have gone far; there was no reason why she should. Nothing had changed - the problem, the threat was still there. I still didn't have any idea what to do. The sex had been very good and yet I was not feeling very happy about it. The past still hung about like a desultory October cloud, dull and uneasy.

I pulled on the boxers-jockey shorts are said to be bad for the 'whatsits' - and went down to the kitchen. She was sitting up at the counter looking a touch petulant, tousled, but undeniably gorgeous in the pink shirt.

"So" I said conversationally. "Here we are."

She did not appear to be impressed by the gambit. Already I could feel her control system coming into play. I knew how tough and manipulative she could be. I took a firm grip on things.

"Gabriella, we now have to do something; we can't just let

this thing ride. You've got to talk to Gary. If it is as dangerous as you and he seem to think, you've got to go to the police." But as I said it I knew he wouldn't, couldn't. She knew it too and looked away.

I sighed and went over to the fridge. A large grapefruit juice and some coffee might stimulate the famous grey cells. Gabriella sipped the coffee she was nursing.

"Gary is still away. I can't go home. At least not until he's back I'm just too dammed scared. I need to hide out for a few days."

"Not here." I said almost too quickly. I made it more decisive. "I've got a ton of work getting ready for Monaco: and they - whoever they are - could well look for you here." Gabriella nodded slowly. She was a remarkably beautiful woman. At this time of the morning, no make-up, after a pretty big night, the eyes were crystal clear and the skin smooth and fresh. I looked away quickly.

"What about your cottage?" She asked suddenly. I turned back towards her.

"How do you know about that?" She grinned for the first time that day.

"Ways and means. The lawyers notified me some time after

the divorce".

"Then, I think they bloody well exceeded their brief". I said angrily. Her amused smile told a story.

"Well" she said "I did get on rather well with Anthony and he was always so helpful." Anthony was my lawyer in the divorce. "Anyway" she went on, "couldn't I stay there for a couple of nights until Gary gets back."

In fact I couldn't see any objection, really.

"Maybe we could arrange something. How would you get there? Where is your car?" This time she switched on the moonbeam eyes.

"I was rather hoping you might drive me down."

I knew I was being used - but I couldn't think of any good reason which wouldn't sound spurious. It was Saturday morning and there wasn't much I could do at the office; I needed to be talking to people and they wouldn't be there.

"OK", I said. " What about your things?" "No point going back to the house?"

"That's for sure" she said. "Can I borrow a few things?" We sorted out a sweater, shorts, some shirts and a couple of pairs of boxer shorts. Imagination boggled at the thought of Gabby wearing them. I noticed that she picked my Vuitton grip to pack them in.

The conspiracy theory was getting to me and I looked out from the window - then the door - before we went out briskly to the car. Then I nipped back to put the house alarm on - better safe. I drove out of the Mews gently - no point in making a big scene - still checking around and about for anything suspicious.

We cut back through Kensington to pick up the North Circular, then the M40.

We were soon in the London Saturday morning traffic with nothing more menacing then being cut-up by a Jeep Cherokee displaying early signs of road-rage. I kept my doors locked in case he stopped and had a go at me with a steering wheel lock. We survived.

Soon we were on the motorway and a dab on the pedal soon bought on easy and illegal one hundred plus.

Neither of us said very much during the journey. Gabby munched a Kit-Kat which I picked up when we stopped for fuel. I was too busy thinking, arguing with myself really, about what to do.

By the time I turned off the M40 it was dusk. We wound our way around Oxford and picked up the ring road. At a large Tesco we took on some basic provisions; and Gabby even had the opportunity to by some knickers and jeans. Not her usual brands but better than nothing. Yes, well...

As we came slowly into the quiet village it was dark, very dark. Not much in the way of street lamps or other external illumination. My small Cotswold stone cottage was on the edge of the village on quite a large piece of its own land. No near neighbours to pry.

I took the car gingerly into the drive - it was in serious need of repair. Full of pot holes, stones and loose gravel.

I locked the car, picked up the grip and went up to the door. With the help of my Maglite I located the keyhole and we were in. No complex alarm systems out here.

It had the dampish smell from being closed up for a while but when I switched the lights on I was pretty impressed: I must come more often.

It didn't take long to get settled in. With the heating on it became quite cosy. Gabriella made some smoked salmon sandwiches - perhaps stretching her culinary skills to the ultimate - while I cooled-down in the freezer cabinet one of the bottles of Veuve Cliquot which I had put in the grip.

We had agreed that I would stay the night. It was logical.

But I had to admit that my imagination was becoming frisky at the thought.

We had just about finished the first bottle when she spoke softly. "Dan, I really am sorry that you have become caught up in this. You are a nice guy and people do take advantage - I'm a prime example. But I did feel desperate. What do you think we can do? Is there a way out? And, by the way, it really is

Just about finished between Gary and me. It really was the old story of terrific sex. If someone can give you really deep pleasure and satisfaction - every time - it just gets hold of you; you lose your sense of perspective and the moral issue just doesn't seem to matter. I suppose I knew that Gary was tricky, an unreliable guy and that his business dealings were more than a bit shady. And I am sure he has a lot of other women. He is bloody good in bed. But still he seemed to want me a lot, until the last few months. And recently I think he has just done me as a matter of routine. This threat, his problems have just bought things to a head."

I can't say that this testament to Gary's super stud performance did much for me, but I think she was trying to tell me something, trying to explain. That's the trouble with Gabriella: you know how manipulating she can be but when she says something real, you do want to believe her.

The atmosphere in the room, with the soft lighting picking up the gleam from old furniture and bits of silver, was sweetly heady. My mind was in dilemma. I knew very well that sex was such a mighty force making people in all walks of life behave irresponsible, throwing morals out of the window. You can accept this, it happens. But not to you personally. I still couldn't follow why Gabby who seemed to be so much in love with me preferred to make love with someone else. I sighed and spoke quietly.

"Yep, Gabriella, I think I know what you are saying. It still hurts but over time I have learned to live with it. Now, actions. One, I've got to get hold of Gary tomorrow and set up a meeting of the three of us. I want to know what is really going on and I want to work out some specific moves with him. I suppose I am still not convinced that this is anything like as big or as you or he are thinking it is. So we need to analyse and see just how we can deal with the problem. Two, you stay here for a few days until I've got a meeting fixed. The phone is off but I'll leave my mobile - there's plenty of power left. I'll get off to London first thing tomorrow and see if I can track him down. Are there any special addresses or numbers, apart from the house?"

She thought a minute then went to get her bag. Deeply embedded in the mystery of its Gucci depths she found a small crocodile skin address book. I got out my pencil and found a sheet of paper.

"There is of course his club. I think he probably stayed there. And he goes quite a lot to Langans - dinner and lunch. His favourite place for drinks in the bar at the Dorchester. He has a small apartment quite close to the office - off Baker Street." She turned and looked up at me. "I think it's where he meets his mistress or mistresses. I never went there. But I've got the number and the address." She gave them to me.

"OK, I'll see if I can find him at one of them." I said reflectively.

She nodded and looked at her watch. She raised her eyebrows whimsically.

"Time for bed."

"Look," I said, "there's only one bed, so you go and settle in there. I can sleep on this." I indicated a large Chesterfield.

"No" she said, "I should feel much happier, more relaxed if you would sleep with me." To tell the truth I was easily talked into it. The road to hell. Good intentions.

After the bathroom ritual we got into bed. A large Victorian, genuine, iron frame bed which I inherited from my great-grand mother. The mattress was thick and soft, standing about three feet off the ground. Getting onto it required a certain athletic skill and once up in the stratosphere you felt it was a somewhat precarious perch. We grinned at one another as we climbed up.

"Goodnight" she said and turned out the light. I am not sure how I felt about that. I think I was expecting her to make some sexual move. I would then have rejected this idea saying that it would be really silly to get involved again; so many problems and complications. But then I would have been talked into it. Yes it would be comforting for both of us, and so on.

I lay there next to her and I could feel the sexual tension building up in my body. I cuffed my pillow and tried to get comfortable. But I couldn't settle. My mind began painting pictures of Gabriella in her sleep. Hair tumbled about her face, arm clutching a pillow. One leg curled up as she lay on her side. It was all too much. I moved towards her and let my hand slide experimentally on her body. I didn't quite know which bit I would make contact with but she had got her back turned towards me and it was the warm firm rotundity of her bottom. My hand, apparently on a self seek mission - nothing to do with me, stroked its way up her body under the old shirt she was again wearing. It found her breast. A breast has a unique texture as does the richness under the skin. A marvellous combination of softness and firmness. No wonder implants are a bust. The sensation of touching is every bit as important as the visual effect. Her nipple felt tantalising under the ball of my thumb: A faintly rubbery sensation as it grew and stretched. Nipples are strange. In an aesthetic design competition they would not do well. Yet when you feel that crinkled rose, or suck it slowly, it goes straight to the top of the creative design league table. In fact there is only one small item which gives it serious competition. Which thought led me down the sweeping curve of her spine, sensing its nodules and into the sudden curve over her buttocks. My fingers slid between and she eased her thighs apart. I felt the liquid glow on my finger tips and...

Suddenly the bedroom door crashed open and a brilliant white torchlight blinded me as I turned towards it. A dark figure erupted into the room and as I turned to clamber out of the bed I was grabbed and thrown to the floor. Gabriella begun to scream but I was fully occupied with the shadowy but brawny assailant. Something hard smashed into my head and I felt a red stab of pain. I lay gasping and terrified. Then I heard Gabriella call out again and through a dizzying mist I saw two figures grappling with her. The adrenalin flowed and I somehow jumped up and dived round the bed. They were heavily engaged with Gabriella and I had a moment's advantage. Many, many years ago I had military service in the Paras, and before that I rated black belt in Judo at the University 'Tiger Judokwai' Club. I crashed my elbow into the neck of the guy nearest to me just where the neck joins the spinal column. And for good measure I thrust my knee into the base of his spine and quickly into the back of his bent-knee. He went down to the floor in a spectacular way. I hadn't been in any kind of physical violence for many a long year and the whole thing seemed more TV than real. The second masked man turned quickly and seeing what had happened he reacted very fast with a slicing kick which barely missed my crotch. He overbalanced and this brought him very close. I remembered an old trick: to scrape the edge of your boot down the shinbone and then stamp very hard on the instep. It began well until I realised that he was wearing heavy boots and I was bare-footed. I had lost what initiative I might have had and when someone behind me tapped my temple hard with what must have been a cosh, I just fell out of it – onto my knees.

All I could remember before blacking out, was a serious of heavy kicks and another bang on the head, against the background of Gabriella's cries which seemed a hundred miles away.

Chapter *6*

Through the dark red throb in my head I gradually came to life. I lay for some time teeth clenched, hanging on to consciousness. Somehow I felt that I had to, otherwise I would die. The light became lighter, clearer and painfully I opened my eyes. Without attempting to move my head I swivelled my gaze slowly round the room. It all looked so ordinary. Somehow I had been expecting chaos, all the signs of a great battle. There wasn't even a bedside lamp knocked over. I took a few deep breaths and tried to sit up. It was a bad move all the pain in my head and body seemed to collide and I fell back retching.

I got my breath back and tried again. Somehow I managed to get on my knees. I crawled over to the corner of the bedroom and found the case which I had left there. I knew the local doctor in the village personally and I was hoping he might be able to come round and sort me out. I dialled on my mobile – fortunately his number was logged in. It rang for a long time.

I suddenly realised that it was after midnight.

"Harry Graham speaking". His voice professional but not glowing with joy. "Harry, it's Dan Piercy. I've had a rather nasty accident up at the cottage. I'm really sorry to bother you at this time – I've probably woken you up. But I'm in trouble and I just don't think I can get to you, or to hospital." I think he sighed.

"OK, Dan, I'll be with you in five minutes."

He was, and by then I had part crawled, part stumbled downstairs. I found a blackthorn walking stick which I kept in the cottage and hobbled to the door to let him in.

"Thanks Harry." I said as he came in. He saw my wobbly state and supported me over to the Chesterfield. He stood back and took in my battered state. I suddenly realised that I was naked.

"My God, what happened to you. Hit by a truck?" He knelt down to take a further look and then set about cleaning me up. "I think we had better get you into hospital" he said. "You've got a massive bruise on your bum and hip, fortunately it's a pretty muscular and well covered bit. And cuts and lacerations on your chest and shoulder. I don't think your ribs have gone but they've taken a pounding."

I realised that I had instinctively rolled into a protective ball to shield my tender parts – especially my goollies. He stood up.

"What happened?"

"Harry, it was an intruder. I think he or they, must have broken in expecting the house to be empty. I woke up, started to struggle and one of them whacked me on the head. Then they gave me a kicking and I passed out."

He looked again at the bloody swelling on my head and shone a torch into my eyes.

"You will have a hell of a headache but I don't think you are concussed."

"I need to get back to London." I said slowly. "Do you think the hospital is essential?"

"I really would recommend it" said Harry. "I think you should have a head scan and the ribs x-rayed. Look, you can't go to London tonight. I'll drive you over in your car, you can have the checks done, stay the night under observation and get off tomorrow morning. It's Sunday so you can't be missing too much."

One set of my brain lobes was telling me what a good idea. The other was working overtime, worrying about Gabriella.

They never seem to be in synch. I didn't think she was dead or anything. This was the kidnapping which she had been going on about and which I had been sceptical about. Now this thing was happening for real and I had to work out what to do. I needed time and a clearer head for that. In the end sense won over sensibility.

"OK" I said to him. "OK, Doc, but what about my car?"

He waved his hand reassuringly. "I'll drive you over to the hospital in it; then I'll get a lift back – no problem. Anyway, it's the only chance I'll have to drive a new XKR, supercharged. Don't worry, my insurance will cover it."

We locked up. It was slightly puzzling that there were no signs of break-in. They must have used the old credit card trick to slip the rather ancient spring lock. He installed me in the passenger seat. Truly the way my head was still buzzing I was very glad that I wasn't driving.

He was a useful driver – bit of a car buff which was how we became friendly.

"How about letting the police know", he suddenly said still looking straight ahead.

"Yes, OK", I replied "obviously I must do that. I'm not thinking straight. But there's nothing they could do tonight. So

I'll call the station tomorrow before I leave. I shan't be quite as groggy then. I hope."

This time he turned briefly to look at me rather questioningly but said nothing. It was useful to have him with me. I quickly got through the admittance and met a consultant.

He stayed while the hospital did the check-up. No serious damage was the verdict so they doped me up, tucked me in – the West Indian nurse was pretty but a disciplinarian – and Harry left with my thanks.

In bed I wanted to stay awake to unravel the problem and make some decisions but I had drifted into deep sleep before I could put my mind in gear. The comforting cocoon of starched sheets and plumped-up pillows.

Hospital breakfasts are early and I was soon up and away. I felt a lot better; my headache had gone, I felt more relaxed. A bit sore and stiff but the Jaguar's soft leather bucket seats eased the pain, as did a couple of aspirin, not brufen; I've an idea they can make you sleepy.

I didn't report the attack to the police, far too complicated. I hoped that Harry wouldn't check. But if the police did look round the cottage, most of the stuff left there was mine. Gabriella had brought virtually nothing. A couple of pairs of super market knickers would hardly cause alarm.

The priority now was to talk to Gary and I thought I would try his office first so I went straight to the glittering Headquarters of the multi-million pound empire which he ran. It was in a converted historic building in High Holborn. I showed the garage porter in his sentry-box my F1 identity card – the one that gets me into the inner sanctum of the pit lane – and he was impressed. He opened the barrier and I was into the private car park under the building.

I took the lift up to the reception floor. Typically the receptionist was long blonde haired, pretty with all the curves. One of Gary's babes perhaps?

"Can I help you?" The voice was overlaid with honey but brittle Essex underneath.

"Yes, please." I said as she looked a touch suspiciously at my bandaged head. " I have to see Mr Gary Enders. Can you call him please?"

She went through the I'm not sure that he's in routine but when I began to get annoyed and had put on my assertive persona she capitulated and called through to his office.

The girl who came out from the adjoining corridor was definitely a Gary babe. This one had an Escada skirt and a lot of class. She gave me a cool inspection. Unlike the porter she seemed totally unimpressed by my card.

"Mr Enders is in conference". She announced using the time honoured formula. My head was starting to throb again, my ribs were sore. I was not well disposed to this corporate brush-off.

"Listen, doll", I said sweetly, "you can take it from me that Gary will definitely want to see me. And he certainly is going to see me. Now trot along and tell him that Dan Piercy is here. You've got five minutes, then I'm coming in."

I strolled down the corridor that became even more plush. I found a cluster of fake Barcelona chairs and eased myself into one. I smiled up at the babe, she teetered uncertainly for a minute then went off bristling with low-grade indignation before disappearing through a very high black door. She was back surprisingly quickly, looking rather miffed.

"Please come this way" she said. Her outer office was incredibly smart and hi-tech, brushed aluminium and grey plastic but she led me straight through to Gary. His room was in fact quite plain – simple, very modern minimalist. He came towards me framed by the view over the City from the window behind him. His face was in shadow and I couldn't read his expression. The P.A. disappeared discreetly behind the door.

"Dan" he began, "I'm a bit surprised that you've come to see me here; you could have called so we could meet somewhere." I saw him glance at my head slightly puzzled. We sat down at a low table. I didn't say anything. I just looked at him. He tried again. "Why here? What's wrong with your head?" I stared him straight in the eyes.

"Gabriella has been taken." I said slowly. His head jerked back and his eyes pinched up.

"My God", "My God", he blurted out. "When? How? What happened?" I told him. He looked stunned.

"I told you" he said. "I told you what they threatened."

"Yep," I said, "so you did." Now what are you going to do? I think you've got to go to the police. You just can't take any risks with her life. You must know that."

He shook his head. "That's not going to solve anything. I can't. They would kill her. And it would finish me."

"That's not the point now." I told him angrily. "It's Gabriella who matters."

He started to explain and I knew that really he was right. The police could not do anything and it would put Gabby at terrible risk.

"What sort of contact do you have with these people?" I asked.

"Through Paris. It's quite straight forward. They are involved in quite legitimate commercial activity so contact is quite normal – almost day to day."

"Do you think that they will contact you?" I asked him. He raised his eyebrows.

"I don't really know. I'd say they will but they may feel that they have already given me the message that I have to start performing – getting the key contracts in place." I think I knew what was coming next. "Dan, won't you go and talk to them – for Gabriella? It was a flashback to our meeting at Estoril when this nightmare began, way back in time but in fact only a few days ago.

"What could I tell them, for God's sake? Why should they listen to me?"

Enders got up and went over to the single painting on the pale white wall – a Piper. He moved it aside and in the cliché of B movie thriller there was a small wall-safe. He took a single, slender key on a chain from his trouser pocket; he opened the small stainless steel drawer and took out a folder. He locked the safe up again and brought the file over to me.

"You could take these contracts to them. They are signed and legalised. The business they relate to is TV coverage in Asia – giving them an exclusive four to a five-year stretch from next year when the current contract with another group expires. In a way it is a perfectly straightforward deal but there are some special clauses, rather well disguised, that could open up the opportunity for dominance. Of course, I know that – and now so do you – but no one else could realise the significance. If you could get them to accept these documents as indicative of my intent, they'll probably release Gabriella. That would give more time to resolve things. Since we talked in Portugal, I've been doing some more thinking and I reckon that with a bit more time I can get us out of it."

He licked his lips. Not very pleasant to watch this proclivity of his to lip-licking: I'm surprised his women didn't notice. Then he decided to tell me. "I'm in talks with another Eastern consortium, a tough bunch but legal, or reasonably legal. There are a few poison pills in that contract which could open it up." He pointed to the file on the table. "But I'm certain that the first consortium doesn't know I'm talking elsewhere. The support of the second lot could give me just what I want to take on the Syndicate."

It all sounded extremely dodgy to me. And a bit unlikely, but I knew that clever contract drafting could leave some subtle escape clauses which a top lawyer could exploit later on.

I was probably being an idiot but the thought of Gabriella did it. Seeing her again, being there when she was taken.

"Let's work out the details" I said. I saw the relief in his eyes. But before he could get too excited, I added, "Just one thing. I want a letter from you explaining that I am acting on your behalf to negotiate Gabriella's release and that I am in no way involved nor have any complicity with your activities." I could see him blink but he nodded.

"Yes, OK, of course."

He went round his desk and took a sheet of writing paper. He unscrewed his black fountain pen and wrote for a few minutes. Then he gave me the letter and the envelope. I looked at it and was satisfied with what he had written.

"OK", I told him, "Now let's get on with it."

"Are you going to contact them?" Gary checked his Tag-Heuer generously equipped with buttons and knobs.

"Too late this morning now. But I am pretty sure that I can get them later this evening." He picked up the phone and called through to his P.A. "Miranda, can you contact our headquarters in Paris and arrange for tele-video meeting with Mr Hang Si Len at 8.00 this evening. I'll call him at his apartment. It's to have a quick word about the new contract: yes, that's right. Good."

He put down the phone and after a minute he looked up at me. "I know how you feel about me", he said. I didn't trust the humility in his voice but what the hell. "But I am really grateful to you for helping. I'm sure Gabriella will be OK. There will be no point in hurting her: she's their check on me, I'll meet you at Langans tomorrow – the 12.30 lunch seating. I'll have all the documents, and an air ticket, hotel reservation...,"

"Gary", I answered, "there's no way I can go tomorrow. Monaco is coming up soon and I've got to get everything in place for our 'Britain Leads in Formula One' promotion. Driving down to Monaco in three day's time."

"So, OK, let's meet at Langans tomorrow and you can tell me what has been arranged. I suggest you fix the meeting in Monaco. I'm staying at the Hotel de Paris."

"Listen, I want something definite about Gabby, some announcement that she is OK. Maybe a voice-mail message with a code on it. The restaurant where she and I went to celebrate our engagement. Believe it or not she'll remember that." She would too despite everything which had happened since.

Gary saw me off the premises himself – attracting a faint sniff from babe number uno and a surprised look from babe grade two. Back in my office I began to work feverishly. There really was a lot to be done before the Monaco Grand Prix. I made a lot of telephone calls, sent a clutch of e-mails and even wrote a few old style letters on our heavy quality logo'd letterhead paper. The posh letters were to VIP's asking for their support or participation. Stirling Moss always came up trumps: still doing his bit for Britain.

Working was really a balm. It had to be done but it also helped to take my mind off things, especially the ever-nagging anxiety about my ex-wife. Carolyn came in with the letters to sign. She had also been sorting out my travel arrangements and had my Seacat crossing tickets and hotel confirmed. Quite an achievement around the Monaco GP week – even though I was travelling out a few days earlier than the time of the main rush by teams and fans to get there. But she was always very efficient and in the few weeks we had been working together, I had grown to depend on her organising skills. She kept things going perfectly when I was away. As soon as we had finished all the paperwork I told her to go home. When she took the job we established a flexi time system.

The office felt lonely and quiet when she left. I went and sat in one of the small comfortable armchairs. I leaned back, encouraging my brain to slow down. But nothing doing. Once the buzz of the job – the F1 business – had died down, the image of Gabriella implanted itself and I began a mental wrestling match. The trouble was I didn't really knew who my opponent was. Two things in particular did bother me. How did the kidnappers know we were at the cottage?. It was a secret hideaway of mine. I tried to work out who else knew about it. And why didn't they finish me off?

I got up to leave and just then the phone rang.

"Hello" I said.

"Hello to you" said the lush voice. It sounded good. "I'm out at Silverstone. Off to Monaco tomorrow. I thought we might meet there. Still some unfinished business."

Chapter 7

These days there is a superb motorway from the French Channel ports, which means you can avoid Paris completely going south. Another bonus is that it is almost empty apart from a few GB sticker cars and the occasional Dutch caravan. But even the Dutch hold no terrors on the wide beautiful engineered lanes. They even call it the English Route. It is a joy to drive – although eventually you have to plug into the AutoRoute de Soleil. On that stretch you really have to go motor racing. Even the clapped-out Clios are pushing 170 kilometres an hour ... Lots of tight downhill bends.

In the Jaguar XKR it was a breeze. Hood down, Darrien Miller championship cap and Web glasses. The business. I felt all the magic of driving a superb car over splendid roads across this magnificent country. I started thinking. I am in a way based at Silverstone so it puzzled me that I had not met Kate before although she had explained she had only recently joined O'Horan because of the pop group sponsorship. But I was certainly looking forward to seeing her soon. I was hoping that her meeting with Gabriella at my flat had been forgotten.

As I swept through the always-breathtaking French countryside, it changed from vast pale gold wheat fields, their perspectives disappearing on the horizon, to the smoky blue mountain ranges of the Alpes Maritimes. The small mountain villages tucked into the landscape always looked so inviting. You know instinctively that there will be a small family auberge with a lunch terrace overlooking the valley; hugely tempting, but I had to press on. I had booked a night stop at Aix-en-Provence. The light was amazing – a soft lemon tone; and the sky seemed so wide and high. Each time it gets to me and reminds me that France is a very large majestic country and the sky its awesome cathedral.

As I drove on through deep-cut gorges and-over long viaducts I began to allow some anticipatory thoughts about Kate O'Malley to trickle into my mind again. One part of me had a guilt feeling that to have lustful thoughts was somehow indecent when Gabby was God knows where and in serious danger. One thing I knew about her kidnappers was that they played very rough. I was pretty well back to normal but I still had the scars to show for my brief encounter. The internal debate continued while I dabbed the brake pedal gently going fast into another sharp right hander. Immediately I saw a yellow Ferrari lance past in the lane inside me. The Ferrari pulled over in front about fifty metres further on as we both levelled out onto a long straight section. There was a derisive wave from the drivers side then the Ferrari driver turned on the gas and raced away. OK I thought. Off you go. I was tempted to take up the challenge: I'm a useful fast driver. But no, I thought, leave it. You've got enough on your mind just now.

I reeled off another hundred kilometres and then decided to stop for a coffee and petrol. The traffic density had built up and the journey had become slower and somewhat boring. I turned into a new motoring complex – L'Air de Lamy. As I cruised gently along the entrance road I spotted the yellow Ferrari. It was parked in one of the bays just outside the Caisse. I filled up and parked the Jag in a nearby spot. I walked over to take a look at the car. Hell's bells. A 550 Maranello. No wonder boyo had gone past me like a train. By now my irritation with the driver for the risky inside overtaking had diminished.

"Nice car" I heard the girl's voice behind me. I turned and smiled.

"It certainly is – but not mine." She was eye catching. Smallish, dressed in a white polo shirt and shorts with a very beautiful black face wearing a lopsided grin showing her perfect white teeth. When she spoke again I picked up the American accent although it was not too obvious. I'd spent some time at Harvard and I reckoned it didn't come too far from there.

"Aha" she said " It's a limey"

I hadn't heard that old fashioned pejorative for quite a while. I hammed it up.

"Well actually, young lady, I am British – English in fact. We do occasionally venture abroad don't you know. And actually I think I might have a stab at the origin of your accent."

"What, American you mean? Amazing" she quipped.

"No I might be able to narrow it down a bit closer than that – how about Wellesley College in Cambridge. That's Cambridge, Massachusetts, not the real one." She cocked a stylish eyebrow at me and rolled her huge lovely eyes.

"Not bad. Not bad at all. I'd like to hear more. Do you feel like a coffee? Or would it have to be Earl Grey tea? C'mon."

She led the way into the café area. We stood at a small table and sipped the rich bitter espressos. She paid. In a few minutes we had established that she had been at Wellesley. I knew of it because when I had been at Harvard Business School we had done some partying with Wellesley girls. One of the most posh, most expensive women's colleges in the States.

"I gotta go" she said, "big date tonight in Monte Carlo."

"Huh, Huh", I looked questioningly at her. "Are you going to be there for the Grand Prix?"

"You bet. I'm covering it for an American magazine. I'm a journalist. Are you going to be there?"

"Yes, I am. Bit of an enthusiast, and I do some PR for British cars. Maybe we'll meet there?". She nodded.

We paused at the exit. "Why are you so interested in the Ferrari? Are you thinking of buying one?" she asked.

"No, they're way out of my league. Anyway, I'm a Brit and I drive Brit cars. But the reason why I was looking at that car was because it passed me a-way-back, passed me on the inside round a very tricky bend. The driver must be a lunatic. I think he must have delusions of being a racing driver." She nodded sympathetically.

"Hell, there are a lot of them about on this motorway. It's not only the speed merchants, you also get doddery old guys in racing green Jags." She walked over to the Ferrari and got in. Of course. It was the same derisive wave as she drove off. I smiled philosophically. Another of my heroic failures. A gorgeous girl and I had let her slip through my palms. No name, contact – and somehow she had me feel a wally. In Monaco during Grand Prix week, not even yellow Ferraris are all that uncommon so spotting her again could be tricky. Anyway it was just a casual meeting and she was obviously not at all interested in a doddery old English guy.

It was early afternoon next day by the time I reached Monaco. Most of the armco barriers were in place and some of the stands were up. I had reserved a place in the hotel garage – or rather super-efficient persuasive Carolyn had – and I was relieved not to have the hassle of trying to find somewhere.

I took my case and the lift up to the reception floor and checked in. I hadn't stayed there before but it looked rather impressive. The receptionist – good-looking, multi-lingual according to his name badge – gave me an envelope with the plastic key-card.

I waited until I was in my room and a couple of suits hung up before I opened it. These Armani linen jackets become so creased in suitcases and an English gent has to keep up standards. The message was written on a single thick sheet of blue vellum paper. The directions were succinct.

Be at the restaurant Les Feiulles in Place Marc Briault at 20.00 hours tonight.

I looked at my Rolex, making the customary time allowance and clocked it at 4pm local time.

When I had met Gary at Langans he had told me that a meeting had been arranged with representatives of the syndicate. They were prepared to receive me as his delegate. He said that they claimed to know nothing about Gabby. Possibly the people up-front who dealt with the legitimate business may not have been in the know about the kidnapping. Obviously the fewer people who knew the better. I had wanted some proof that they had Gabriella and she was OK. However, there didn't seem to be much option. I had the contracts which I understood were absolutely authentic, properly signed and witnessed. Gary had told me that I should take the papers to the first meeting and hand them over. After that he promised that Gabriella would be released immediately. But I decided to play it differently. I would take a couple of sheets – the ones with the signatures and official stamps – for them to examine. Then I could set up an exchange for Gabby. There was at least one problem with this brilliant tactic: I had no idea where she was or whether she was in any way near to Monaco. I guessed probably not. But I had to keep some edge of bargaining power.

I decided to get on with some work in the meantime. My first call was to the office of the Autoclub of Monte Carlo which was responsible for the local arrangements. My credentials were good and they invited me round. It was a rather old world office away from the centre.

I was fascinated by the black and white signed photograph of Louis Chiron in a Bugatti, Circa 1935 I reckoned. White linen wind cap and big chrome goggles. The real thing.

The negotiations for the British position at the race had been agreed in advance. There would be a lunchtime demonstration before official practise on the Saturday.

An impressive parade of British past motorsport Grand Prix winners – Lotus, Cooper, Vanwall, B.R.M. also Jaguars and Aston Martins from the Le Mans 24 hours race. Quite a few British personality drivers: great names from the past and some more recent names. Although I say it myself, I knew it would be a splendid very impressive affair. All the world's top press had been alerted; there would be a press photo call and TV interviews on the F1 network. Our other coup was to be providing an official course car. The new small Jaguar. It was up rated in performance because for the warm-up lap, or during yellows, it really had to go quickly to avoid holding the racers back and possibly causing over-heating. The final touch was that all the support vehicles were British 4x4s.

The guys in the organiser's office were really very nice and helpful. I had thought they might resent this Brit stealing their show but not a bit. In fact, there seemed to be a lot of enthusiasm for the old British Racing Green even though they are puzzled because it is almost black. They invited me to the annual club dinner that night – part of the Grand Premier celebrations but of course I had to decline gracefully because of the rendezvous with the syndicate. Back at the hotel I booked a taxi to take me to the restaurant.

It was nice to luxuriate in a big bath in a classy old style hotel. Lots of fluffy towels. Then I got ready to go out. The sample sheets of the contract I folded neatly and pushed into the inside pocket of my dark grey linen jacket. I took the briefcase containing the remaining sections of the contract with me down the reception and had them put into the hotel safe.

Mind you, you always wonder how safe hotel safes are. When I gave my room number to the receptionist she took a note from the pigeonhole. "Madame Kate O´Malley called when you were on the telephone; she said she would call later". The receptionist struggled a bit with O'Malley but I knew very well who it was. I thanked her and went out to find my taxi.

The restaurant was a long way from the centre in a part of Monte Carlo I had never before been to. It was a pretty seedy area which somehow did not fit with the image of the glamorous principality. But all towns and cities have to have less expensive areas for the people who actually do the work. I got out of the taxi, paid him, and he drove away. I looked around, cobblestone square with very old-fashioned wrought iron street lamps; not many of them so there were a lot of dark patches. It was very much the setting for a second-world war spy drama with the Gestapo and flicks suddenly roaring round the corner in large Mercedes saloons and Citroens *tractions avants*. It was that vivid imagination of mine again. I opened the door of the restaurant Les Feuilles and strode manfully inside. There was a small bar overhung with a canopy liberally decorated with various bunches of leaves. I was in the right place. A waiter in classic attire come forward, black trousers, white shirt, black waistcoat, black moustache and naturally the long white apron almost down to the floor.

"Monsieur?" he said. Just that. Before I could reply a man moved out from one of the tables. In fact he seemed to be the only other person in the place. He held out a large nicely manicured hand.

"I'm Fred Lenski Junior. And I know that you're Dan Piercy. I've seen your photograph. Good likeness. Why don't we just sit down over here, have a drink?"

I'm not sure quite what I was expecting but it wasn't this. He looked exactly like a successful affluent American corporate lawyer. Brooks Brothers clothes, large welted brogues and rather short trousers. I followed him to the table.

"Ricard", I said to the waiter before either of them could ask. Fred smiled approvingly.

"OK" he said, when the drink had appeared. "Cheers." He touched his glass of red wine to mine. I remained thoughtful. He probably assumed I was a tight-arsed Brit.

"I am here as the attorney of a certain syndicate. I'm real sorry about this set-up here, but we wanted it to be a nice quiet meeting. We do some business with the proprietor here and he kindly let us have the use of this room for an hour.

Anyway, his usual clients come in later." I didn't respond at all. He pushed on.

"As I understand the position from my client you will be handling over to me some documents concerning a major transaction which has been agreed. So I guess we can do that part and then have a nice old drink together."

His affability was in contrast to his eyes. They were very dark brown, almost black and quite expressionless. It was wrong to make snap judgements on people but I was prepared to place a large bet that in this case the first impression was probably sound. I did not take kindly to this American lawyer.

"Mr Lenski", I said evenly. "That may be the arrangement which you have in mind, but it isn't what I have in mind. I'll try to put this diplomatically. There is another important aspect to the deal. The young lady who has been staying with your friends has to get back to her job. She was supposed to be here this evening so that I could give her a lift home. It was a convenient arrangement since I would be meeting you to present the contract papers. But I don't see her. Has she been delayed?" Of course I knew that Gabriella was not going to be there, to be handed over at that meeting. But I wanted to get a reaction – to establish that part of the deal.

"Hell, Dan, I didn't hear anything about a lady – just to pick up the contract. So what do you say we get on with it. Where is it by the way? You don't seem to have any file with you." He had a curious mannerism of rolling his head sideways as he spoke, slipping a plump finger into the edge of his button-down collar.

"I'm afraid that's not on. No ladyfriend, no contract." I shook my head at him and raised my shoulders and arms in a little Yiddish play-acting. He was still smiling, just.

"Heh, we don't seem to be making much progress here. I suggest you just give me the documents and we'll be in touch about any other matters." There was a strong tension in the air now. Mr Lenski was not a happy bunny and it was starting to show. I let things remain static for a minute.

"I can cut a deal" I said, "how about this?" I'll give you a specimen just to show good will, and so that you can check the authenticity. Then we fix a date and place – I'll choose it – where I'll give you the rest of the contract papers and you deliver the lady in question. No more crap – that's it." I took a quick look at my watch – nearly 8.15pm. We'd been talking like this for a quarter of an hour.

The lawyer lit a Camel and exhaled slowly.

"Mr Piercy". Good old Dan was out of it. "Mr Piercy, I don't think you are being very smart. The people you are dealing with don't like games. They get bored quickly. They are not going to like your attitude in this matter. Our information from Mr Enders was that you were just the courier. Perhaps you don't get what your role is."

"Stuff Mr Enders" I told him. "The way it is now, I'm calling it." I took the folded papers from my inside pocket and passed them over the table. "These are the samples. Check them out and let me know when you are ready to do the exchange."

He took them, gave them a cursory glance and slid them into a small case which I now saw he had on the chair beside him.

"You are a real fucker", he said now openly angry. "The people will not like this. They will kick my arse. I reckon you need a lesson not to play with big boys. You're way outa your league." He turned to the back of the room. "Viktor."

A tall man with pure white hair cut en brosse came out of the shadows. Lenski pointed at me.

"Hurt him. Make him remember it. Just enough for him to remember who he's dealing with." Lenski then waved to the waiter – who could have played the classic sinister butler a treat – to lock the restaurant door.

I have to admit to a certain anxiety. Only recently I had been on the wrong end of a beating-up. But, right on cue, before the waiter reached the door it swung open and four noisy blokes, sounding for all the world like the dreaded English lager louts, pushed in. It was my insurance policy. I had taken the precaution of phoning Jonathan Piercy who had arrived ahead of his Johnson Racing team mates. He played some rugby before he found his real talent as a racing driver and he always invited some ex rugby club mates – special friends – to some of his races. Monaco of course was a favourite. I had suggested that they meet me for a drink at Les Feuilles about 8.15pm. Johny knew that there might be trouble but not why.

Blondie, Fred and the sinister waiter looked at them. One of Jonathan's pals was a big number eight over six feet five inches tall. Another was a prop forward giving the impression of being six feet wide. What did it, was when Johny, who was genuinely a top class clay-pigeon shot – opened a brown case he was carrying and pulled out, part way, an under-and-over shot gun. He slapped a box of shells in front of him and broke open the breech.

"What d' you think Dan" he said enthusiastically. "Just picked it up. The F1 drivers are having a charity competition shoot after the race and I decided to get a bit of practise." He looked at Lenski and the white haired heavy as if he had only just noticed them.

"Hello", he said sweetly, "sorry to be rude. Are these friends of yours Dan?"

"Sort of", I said, "but we only just met and I think they were just leaving. We may be doing some business together in future though."

Johny idly slipped a shell into the breech, pulled it out, slid it again as though he was testing it.

"Oh, that's a shame", said Ben, the prop forward. "I thought perhaps we could all have a few jars together. Your new friends look as though they could be great company."

Ted Lenski sighed and nodded at blondie, who relaxed a bit. "Dan's right, we do have to leave now. But, Dan, we'll be in touch real soon. Now you take good care, real good care."

He nodded briefly at the barman who was looking spaced out. They left.

"Jonathan" I said, "your timing was perfect. And I liked the gun bit. I have to tell that our blond friend was probably armed and a professional thug."

"Ah, I'd say he was a poufter" quipped Ben. "He'd have his professional arse well kicked playing against West Hartlepool. But what about the drinks then? Jonathan swore there would be a few pints going if we came to your party."

"I'd say we can find somewhere more congenial", I answered him, feeling a lot more cheerful, "but before we leave I'm sure that our friendly barman could do us a few litres of Soixant cent seize quatre."

"What the hell's that? Sounds like a new filthy sex position." Ben again. He was the funny man and with his persuasive charm and seventeen stones I'd challenge anyone not to laugh. Even the barman was trying to raise a smile.

"M'sieur", I said to him grimly, "Cinq grandes biers, Knonenbourg, pression, vitement, s'il vous plait."

We downed the beers, chatting and laughing like a bunch of boys on the town. We had another round. And another. Then we decided to find somewhere more cheerful. "A wee bit of company" as Alisdair, the number eight put it. We left. We didn't pay. The barman didn't mention it. He looked relieved to see us go.

The lads had walked and they knew the way back to

civilisation. Although it seemed a rough area nobody gave us any bother. They were wise. I dropped a couple of paces behind with Jonathan.

"Thanks again", I said.

"Don't you dare mention it, ever" he said. "You've been the best to me. I certainly wouldn't be where I am in F1 without you." He turned towards me. "And as a matter of fact there is a problem I'd like to talk over with you soon. I've had more than enough to drink; any chance we could go back to your hotel for a quick chat? The lads can go on the booze – but I'll ask Alisdair – he's the sophisticated one – to keep his mobile on. Just in case."

Twenty minutes later we were in my room. Jonathan, me and the Browning automatic shotgun.

Chapter 8

I had ordered some coffee and we chatted inconsequentially until it had arrived. Then Jonathan began.

"It's about next season", he said. I looked up at him sharply. "I thought you had a two year contract at Johnson Racing?"

"Yes, I do and I'm very happy about it. They have been giving me terrific support and my race engineer is great. We get on well and he's a real pro. I've been getting some very good results – on the podium for every race so far this year including a win."

"So, what's the problem, Jonathan?"

"I've been getting repeated offers to join another team – one of the new Asian teams. They were offering me a fortune, three times what I'm earning now, plus an amazing sponsorship package. It seems that the money bags, the consortium behind the team is a conglomerate with interests in a whole range of industries' – clothing, toiletries, vitamin foods, drinks, the lot. I told them no thank you. I'm under contract and I am very happy where I am. But they keep on contacting me. People are beginning to notice it and the motor sport writers are starting to speculate that I'm in negotiation with another team. I suspect that the Asian team may have planted a few indiscreet items of press gossip. You know what it's like at this time of the year. Everyone is talking about driver changes and if there isn't any hard news you can always make up a tasty item. And there's another thing. I got the impression that the Ring Master himself – Gary Enders – thinks that it is a good idea." He took a breath, then looked straight at me. "Dan, he took me to a very good dinner a couple a weeks ago and told me that it could be good for my career, that Johnson Racing was stagnating like some of the other traditional teams and if I was smart I would make a move now and get in on the new wave." He paused. "Gary also said he had discussed it with you and although you didn't want to get directly involved because of your job, you thought it was a great idea. But he asked me to keep that to myself so as not to embarrass you. So I'm sorry if I'm putting my foot in it now but I am really worried and wondering what to do. Not a good scene for a race driver."

I was worried as well by what he just told me. It all added

up. Gary was starting to get drivers in place for the new Asian teams.

"Jonathan, I can't tell you everything but I want you to be aware that there are some very serious problems at the moment in Formula One. I hope that they will soon be sorted out. I'm not directly involved but I am unfortunately caught up in it to some extent. But I can tell you this - I have never discussed your career with Gary. So he's lying when he says that I think a move from Johnson Racing would be a good idea. On the contrary I think it would be crazy; when the new engines become available they'll be hard to beat. My advice is stay with your present team. I don't like Enders, I don't trust him an inch and I advise you not to either. It was very different when Ben was in charge. But Gary Enders is from a different planet and he has a totally different agenda. Keep this to yourself at present. I'm involved in some tricky negotiations. In fact, tonight's little episode was part of it. The people involved are very unpleasant t and tough. I hope I can sort it out – because someone's life is in danger, as bad as that – but if I can't get it settled soon I shall have to go to the police and the authorities. Now back to you. My advice is to talk with your boss. Tell him exactly what is happening, how you're being pressed to join another team but that you don't want to leave Johnson Racing. Make it clear that you are not just angling for a pay-rise. Explain that all the publicity is phoney. You have every intention of honouring your contract and you hope he wants you to stay."

"Man", said Jonathan. "Sounds very murky. But thanks for telling me Dan. I feel a lot happier now about my side. I'll talk to Johnson Racing as soon as they get here. But what about you? Now, that worries me. Promise you'll tell me if ever you need help. Especially if you need any physical back up. As you can see I can pretty well field a full rugby fifteen." He was clearly anxious but he managed an encouraging grin.

We talked a bit longer. I promised Jonathan that I would let him know immediately if I needed any kind of help. He insisted on giving me his mobile number. He seemed in much better spirits when he left. I got the feeling that he was glad to have cleared his mind about the problem of changing teams; now he could concentrate on the forthcoming race. And I must admit from my perspective it was good to know that he and his rugby friends were there. I wondered what the next move by the syndicate would be. I wondered who they were? All I had from Gary was the vague notion of a group of Asian business interests. But there had to be real people, actual companies behind it. If offers were being made to drivers it couldn't be long before teams were announced. There must be some commercial infrastructure - legal entities in place already. Some corporate groups registered. I could ask Gary but I knew for certain that he would fob me off. I thought it would be no harm to do a bit of my own research. Tomorrow I would make a few phone calls.

I wasn't too worried now about Gabriella. There didn't seem to be any point in their harming her. They already had a lot on Gary – she was just a symbol, a reminder. But the way they quickly resorted to violence – the threat to me in the restaurant – was worrying. It seemed a knee-jerk response to any kind of opposition. But that didn't fit with the idea of an all powerful semi–legitimate business syndicate. The obvious explanation was that they were using intermediaries to distance themselves from any unpleasantness.

I was jotting down a few names and 'must do' notes on my pocket pad when the doorbell rang. I felt a spasm of fear, then relaxed. They wouldn't be crazy enough to try anything here. Nevertheless I went to the wardrobe where Jonathan had left his Browning shot gun. The cover for me to keep it was an entry acceptance in the charity clay-pigeon competition and I had all the support documentation. I slid a shell into the breech and left it open just under the bed valance. I looked through the spy-hole in the door. The magnifying effect gave a tall long visual of a woman. I could guess. When I opened the door Kate was leaning against the jamb, an elegant arm on the hip and one leg stylishly crossed over the ankle of the other.

"Now, why didn't you tell me you were staying at the Hotel de Paris, and me booked at the Hermitage?" she asked in the almost familiar soft voice with an eye arched at an impossible angle. "Anybody would think you were trying to avoid me." Once again, she pushed her way easily through the door way and as I stepped back she gently closed it. She smiled, and kissed me on the mouth. It was sweet but raw brown sugar not refined white. I liked it a lot. Almost without pausing, she moved over to the desk and picked-up the hotel phone.

"This is room 366. Can you please send up a bottle of Veuve Cliquet, non-vintage, very cold, and two glasses, please?" Kate always seemed to hypnotise me. She made all the moves. I stood there like a supporting role actor. So she sauntered over to me and stood incredibly close. Just the nearness of this stunning beauty brought a very strong reaction.

She smiled knowingly,

"So you are pleased to see me – or is that a bottle of champagne in your trouser pocket?" It was a corny old joke but she made it live again. The door buzzer went and broke the spell momentarily. The waiter was there with the cooling bucket and a champagne top sticking up from the ice. Very cold she said. Cold it was.

"M'sieur, M'dame". The waiter walked over to the table. He opened the champagne neatly and then presented me with the bill to sign. It was set off handsomely by its silver and enamel presentation box. I dropped a fifty franc note in to keep it company. I could sense that the waiter was in favour of this move.

"Merci, bon soir M'sieur, M'dame."

I quickly poured two glasses of the fizz and gave her one. It was deliciously cold. Wine buffs would disagree but I insist that white wine should be ice-cold. Kate drank most of her glass quickly and put it down. She turned off the main light leaving just a soft glow from the large table lamp. Her next initiative held my attention. She reached behind her and slid down the long zip of the clinging filmy dress she was wearing. Perhaps I should say had been wearing because in one graceful movement she had slipped it down and stepped out of it. She looked terrific in her burgundy lace underwear. It had that special very feminine, very expensive cut. So did she. But in a twinkle of an eye both wispy items were off and Kate was down to her own resources, which were stupendous. Her breasts were full and firm, nipples stretching out invitingly, shoulders rounded, graceful slender arms, her stomach curving down to the mound of glossy deep red pubic hair, and then the incredibly long well shaped legs flowing from full curved hips and taut high bottom. My God, what a package. From then on my intellectual faculties faded out and sheer physical desire took over.

We had begun a nice flirtation in the Tivoli Jardim bar when I had been hoping for a bit of action, but now I couldn't really see why she seemed so determined to get me into bed. Mind you, I was not complaining... She tiptoed naked over to me and pressing everything against me she kissed me long and deep. I kicked off my shoes unaided. Shirt, belt, trousers, pants were soon disposed of. I was naked, very erect and hard. Kate turned, clasped her hand round the shaft of my penis and led me to bed.

She was an incredible lover. Sitting astride she used her

body to tease and thrill. Small short movements round the tip, then long deep plunges. As I came for the third and final time all my nerve endings were stretched to breaking point as I thrust hard in the final strokes. She fell asleep quickly, rolled onto her side. I lay awake for some time. I replayed the scene in my mind. It had been a unique experience. Totally animal though. She seemed feral in her demands. But were there any feelings of affection? Love?

I wasn't to find out this trip. When I woke she was gone. On the bottom of my wallet note pad, she said scrawled,

Must do this to you again sometime. See you. K.

I wondered.

After a quick croissant and coffee I got to work to improve my database on Asian automotive dealings. First, I called a guy I knew at Brightwell Consulting - he specialised in Pacific Rim Business and had spent a lot of time in Japan, Korea and Taiwan. I knew he couldn't divulge anything too specific or confidential. We were pretty good mates – we had roomed together at Harvard - and I reckoned he would be willing to give me some idea of any major activities. We talked for a while and I told him roughly what I was interested in. I gave him the Formula One background, and knowing my new role in promoting British motor racing interests he understood why I was being nosey about the developments in the Far East motor scene. He said he had heard a few rumours and promised to follow them up. I arranged to call him at the end of the week. The next call was to Professor Deryck Morgan at the Coventry Polytechnic Business School – an expert on the automotive world. He was very knowledgeable about international strategies of the major multi-nationals. He and I collaborated in the past on some in-depth research preparing reports for some pretty big names. I think I had been able to help him quite a lot on the motor racing point of view for a study he had done for the UK auto industry about the affect of Britain's motor racing success on the specialist auto companies. He was lecturing when I called but his assistant Elizabeth, who sounded really nice, took detailed notes and promised that she would get back to me.

I was thinking about my next move when the bedroom telephone rang. It was Gary. He didn't sound happy. Seemed to have lost his cool.

"What the hell are you playing at?", he blurted over the

phone. "I've had them on to me and they are furious about last night's little pantomime. It has made the situation very sensitive. They hate losing face; they think you made them look foolish."

I was expecting this reaction from him but that didn't make it any easier to take. I was feeling pretty annoyed myself.

"Shut up" I said, "and listen to me. You got me into this mess and if you don't like the way I am handling it then I'm out, now. And I'll go straight to the police. You told me that Gabriella would be released after the exchange of the documents. Well, there was no sign from them that that is on their agenda – now or in the future. I don't think she is in France – or Monaco, anyway. As it worked out I was quite rightly suspicious and gave them only specimen documents just to keep something up our sleeve. So let me turn your question around. What the hell are you playing at? You seem to me telling me one thing and then giving in to them. The thing is I don't believe that Gabby is your priority: you are more concerned with saving your own skin – your own business reputation - not to mention the money involved."

He was quiet for a long minute. I could almost sense him getting himself under control. Probably he was physically putting on a soothing smile. He needed me and he couldn't afford to alienate me.

"Yes, yes, OK", he said eventually. " I can see how it all went wrong. But why did you bring that gang of football hooligans? That's what upset the American lawyer."

"Well, for one thing", I said mildly now, "they happen to have been some old friends – not soccer hooligans; and for another I had already arranged to meet them for a drink when I got the message. So it was easier to suggest that they came to the restaurant rather than put up complicated excuses. As it worked out, I was glad to have them there. The yank and his blond heavy were proposing to beat the shit out of me for annoying them. Who is blondie anyway? Do you know?."

Again the pause. Thinking. "Dan, I didn't want to say too much about this before but I think they've got the Russian – Moscow- Mafia fronting for them. They provide the hard face and the association keep well in the background, very legal and proper. And I believe it's the Russian team which is holding Gabriella. That's why we have to be so careful not to get it wrong in the negotiations. Those guys are vicious and if there are any problems the quick way is to get rid of her. They would still have plenty to blackmail me with."

"I had a feeling the big white haired guy was Russian and I

also sense that he was one of the kidnap team. Something about the way he moves." I said, but Gary Enders didn't pick up on this. He wanted to move on.

"Honestly Dan, the best thing all round is to give them the remaining papers and we can set up Gabriella's release. I can do that – I know – if you give them the contract. I don't think she's anywhere near you either. So there's no way they could meet your demand. Let me talk to them, assure them that you will give them the full contract, and get a promise of an early release for Gabriella wherever she is. Of course, they'll want a guarantee that she'll keep quiet, but I think she'll go along with it because if she doesn't, I'll be finished anyway and being poor is not one of her best things."

"Uh, uh", I replied," I agree. "But I want to speak to her first. Get them to arrange for her to give me a quick call here on my mobile." I gave him the number. "They can leave a message with the time for the next meeting; not during practise; I'm on duty then. One other thing. Tell them I shall leave a letter in the hotel safe explaining where I have gone to deliver the documents and why. So if anything unpleasant happens to me there will be some pretty serious repercussions." Actually there was a lot of bluff in that threat because there wasn't much factual evidence that I could put in the letter. But it was something.

I didn't discuss Jonathan's situation with him. Something told me it was better to keep Jonathan out of this. Enders said he would set everything up and rang off. I still had a job to do so I packed a briefcase and left the hotel.

At the race control centre I the found Jaguar head of sport. We had a look at the special version which was going to be used as a pace car to lead the cars round on their warm-up lap. I checked all the decals and the special equipment which had been fitted. The scrutinisers would also test it before practise began.

My other priority was to make sure that the fleet of cars to be driven round the circuit by British celebrities was here and that all the admin was in place. The collection of UK built cars looked good. Astons, Jags, Lotus, TVR, MG and Bentley. The VIP drivers had already had a test run at Brands Hatch which is a pretty twisty tight little circuit, so there shouldn't be any problems. Certainly not by the collection of ex-world champions we had lined up to drive for Britain!

The teams were settling in and I took a stroll round the very restricted pits area. Space is at a premium everywhere in

Monaco. I put my nose into the Mac Cracken garage, but not very far. The Chief Engineer has a clear policy: no outsiders, no one gets inside their garage. Very understandable. The motor home is a different and I was made welcome there. These are very glamorous places these days where the seriously high-value F1 team drivers can be cosseted in between practise sessions. A sanctuary from the pressure of publicity demands, the fans, and where they can try to deal with their own devils. Why do I brake too early for Casino?. How can I save one hundredth of a second through Racasse. A millisecond too soon and we finish up in the Armco.

A place too for the team boss to meet a journalist and explain why the team had problems at the previous Grand Prix and why it's going to do better later on in the season. Massaging the sponsor's egos.

Yes don't let's forget the sponsors. Without them there would be no Formula One as we know it today. The motor home is where they can entertain their very privileged clients as well as being entertained themselves by the team bosses they're sponsoring. This is a very hierarchical world. A rich mixture of very big business and top international sport with large financial rewards. Inevitably this breeds serious competition and some rough, tough machinations between all the parties involved. Drivers looking for top money and the best car to win in; teams scheming to get the best drivers and also those who will attract or bring with them the most lucrative sponsorships; teams and sponsors playing games against the background of the tobacco world; and designers and engineers trying to get every once of advantage from the regulations without actually breaking any rules – or at least being found out. An every day life of modern sponsorship. Trouble is I still love it, warts, wrinkles, tits and bums, Gary Enders and all. I finished my coffee, thanked the Mac Cracken boys and moved on.

One of the reasons I love it is the whole damn colourful scene. Beautiful cars, beautiful people, beautiful bottoms. There we are again. Female pulchritude rears its lovely behind. Formula One does attract the babes. The money of course is a pull. But it is also the place to be seen for an aspiring super-star. In fact there were a lot of photographers with press passes milling around and I noticed one from a high fashion magazine which is –not exactly a serious motor sport publication. A lot of them would be cleared out of the pit area by the time practise began. As an enthusiastic follower of fashion I noticed an interesting theme. A lot of the girls were wearing short filmy little skirts instead of trousers or shorts. Very nice the way in which they just float and flick round the hips swirling, always promising to show a little more thigh, or even a flash of knickers, but so cleverly cut that they show nothing extra. But it is pleasantly tantalising to hope.

There was a special crop of celebrities at Monaco. It is the smartest Grand Prix of the whole season: Monaco is that kind of place. At Monaco the real pits are not much more than a strip of tarmac; and they are some fifty metres from the paddock which is on the quayside on the opposite side of the harbour to the chicane. So all the motor homes and huge vehicle transporters are all parked a fair distance from the pit lane. All the equipment – and the F1 cars themselves – have to be wheeled along the pits each time before practise, an the race. Of course, this is totally anachronistic by modern standards and is only accepted by the teams because everyone knows that Monaco is magic, is unique. The place to be seen is the Paddock Club and fortunately my badge and pass would get me in.

I waved to Pete at Johnson Racing. I thought about Jonathan and the team contract. I hoped that he would soon have a chance to talk to his boss and make sure he knew the true situation. As I came up to a green-yellow garmented group from O'Horan I suddenly thought about Kate. At Estoril I had been hoping to see her. Now at Monaco, after our session, I didn't feel quite the same. She was a fantastic female; visually, physically, mentally and a tigress in bed. But I just didn't feel that touching of hearts. Call me old-fashioned but although no one enjoys lusty sex more then I do, I think it is one hundred percent better when 'lurve' walks in. That's all I had ever really wanted – one special woman to be in love with for eternity. 'Yuck' as Gabriella would say.

Damien was being interviewed by a top TV network and looked in very good form with a new short haircut and a confident grin. He was so much more relaxed now that he had a successful car again and had regained his winning ways. He waved at me and pointed at the cap he had given me a year back.

"You need to buy a new one", he called out. "Can't you see we have changed the design." He pulled the peak of the cap he was wearing. Then he took it off and threw it over to me.

"Here, you'd better have this. We can't have the British F1

representative in the wrong livery."

"Ta", I grinned back, swapping over the caps. "Good luck."

There were two other teams which were doing better now - both run by former drivers. The Johnie Ewart team had recently got a virtually brand new engine and signed with Scots Donald Coltherne and Mario Forzett; the latter back from the States after winning a major championship. Ecurie Prens had found a new brilliant young French driver. Whatever was said otherwise that team really ought to have a French leading driver. The new guy was called Remy Farce-Ponte; a helluva name but a helluva driver and he had the looks and style to go with it. He was already being featured in car ads and for a men's cologne promotion on French TV.

Mac Cracken had also returned to their position as top players. Schwarzkopf could do well for them here. At Monaco he either drove a blinder, one of his mind-boggling exhibitions of car control, or ran into the barrier early in the race.

I carried on my tour making sure that all the Brit teams – which is in fact most of the teams – were flying the special flag with the 'Britain leads in F1' logo, and were dishing out publicity material, t-shirts and stickers. There was a press meeting set up for lunchtime so I made my way back to our small marquee near the Paddock Club.

I was pleased to see that a lot of motor racing journalists had turned up, not just British, but from all over. I'd got a few VIP personalities to circulate and massage the glamour side of the story. The Secretary of State for Trade and Industry, the British Ambassador, the Minister for sport and the Earl of Highgate who had recently re-opened the wonderful, nostalgic, Roundwood circuit were all there. Quite a few racing drivers past and present had also turned-up. At least the business side of my life was doing well even if my personal life was full of problems. I made a short announcement explaining what my role was and why we were promoting Britain's leading role in motorsport. It was done in the right language for motoring writers, crisp, giving factual information and delivered without notes, although I had rehearsed it several times to get the off-the-cuff style right. At the end I invited them all to the champagne lunch and to the special reception that night which involved all the British teams. I took a few questions – fairly straightforward. Then from the back of the press area a voice which I recognised said,

"How do you justify calling all those cars you'll be parading tomorrow as British? Most of them are owned by foreign groups. I mean, c'mon." It was my friend from the encounter on the French auto-route, the yellow Ferrari flyer, American journalist Holly Bright. She stood up and looked at me challengingly but with a glint of humour in her eyes and her quirky smile.

"Final ownership of almost all major business today is multi-national." I said looking serious but game playing with her. "The only way you can determine the nationality of a car is on the basis of where final assembly takes place. So just for the record, Jaguars are built in Britain. So are Aston Martin cars, MG, Bentleys and of course some of the leading Honda, Nissan and Toyota models. Britain is also a major producer of top quality auto components, all of which benefit from the impact of motor racing development. One of these days I'd like to see passenger safety cells developed from the ultra-strong composites which protect F1 drivers. That would be a great benefit to standard cars stemming directly from British F1 technology." I sat down. She stood up.

"Well if these Brit cars are so good why is that you get one being driven so slowly in the fast lane of French motorways by an ultra-slow Englishman?."

A lot of heads turned towards her; then back at me. A bit like a Wimbledon tennis rally. I took up the challenge, then closed her down.

"May I suggest that British cars, like British drivers, are not flashy and exhibitionist. They perform to the maximum only when necessary. And on that high note, ladies and gentlemen, may I invite you to the champagne."

There was a determined, though not aggressive move towards the bar. A pleasant melée followed. A few journalists – mostly British – sounded about as impressed as hard-bitten correspondents could ever sound. I felt quite pleased. But we'd have to wait to find out what they had actually written. I looked around for Holly Bright but she had obviously not waited for the champagne.

As soon as the lunch was over I left the circuit and went back to the hotel. My day-job was over now, I wanted to see what news there was of Gabriella if any. There was a message simply saying that there would be another call at 2.30pm and a further one at 5pm. It was just after 2.15pm when I got to the room. I sat down for a nail-biting wait. Bang on 2.30pm the telephone rang. I picked it up and said,

"Hello, this is Dan Piercy."

There was a delay of a couple of seconds, then Gabriella's voice,

"Hello Dan, this is really me." She told me where we had celebrated our engagement. "Dan, I can only speak for a bit. I'm OK, really. In fact I have been pretty well looked after. But I am frightened of what might happen if you upset them again. So please do what they ask. And Dan, I ..." Her voice suddenly disappeared and an accented male voice took over.

"Be at the heliport at Loews at 3.15. Bring the documents. No games this time. If the contract is OK she will be released." The line disconnected.

I looked at the trusty Rolex, 2.35pm. Time enough to get to the Heliport even with the traffic density. I was puzzled because the voice which instructed me was in the same location as Gabriella. But I felt sure that they weren't holding her anywhere near Monaco. But of course the call could have come from anywhere. There were almost certainly at least two groups involved – probably more.

OK. I would play it straight up. I couldn't see how it would achieve anything to try to insist on some other arrangement. I went down to the reception, had the contract file taken out of the safe and replaced by the self-protection letter. I got the posh doorman in his tailed coat and tall hat to find me a cab. I thought he had a better chance of plucking one out of the traffic flow than little old me. I was right. A fifty-franc note changed hands as I stepped in. Zooming through the famous tunnel is always a reminder of how demanding the changes of light in such a tight narrow space must be when you are racing through it at more than one hundred and forty.

It didn't take long to get to the Heliport. I was at least ten minutes early. But I was quite happy to have a few minutes' opportunity to scout-out the land. I took the lift up to the deck. There was a small lounge. A few businessmen who looked quite normal; and a rather prosperous gent in a yachting blazer and white trousers. No one seemed to be interested in me. I wandered around and finished up looking out over the landing circle through a panoramic window. I glanced at the futuristic clock pulsing away its digital minutes. Just as the thirty-minute number came up I heard the clack of the chopper blades and a pale blue machine came down into the circle, its slipstream driving dust up against the window. I watched as the blades slowed to a lazy rotation. The side door opened and a slightly built Asian male got out and dropped neatly onto the tarmac. As he came into the lounge I saw him looking around. Almost immediately he picked me up and walked briskly towards me. He was in an unobtrusive outfit: dark blazer and slacks, white shirt and striped tie.

"Mr Piercy", he said as he came up to me. I nodded. "Would you like to come with me, sir? It's just a short flight out to the company yacht. I shall expect to bring you back again by 4.30pm at the latest." He kept his voice down. I looked at him for a reflective minute.

"Ok" I said, "You know my rules."

We went out together to the helicopter. I saw him looking at the slim pigskin case I was carrying – the one Gary had originally given me to transport the contract. We ducked instinctively under the blades. We strapped ourselves in and the pilot took us straight up before swinging tail-up in a long slow loop out over the startling blue of the Med.

It was interesting to get this birds-eye view over the circuit, which could be seen quite clearly amongst the normal street pattern, as it cut down to the water front. Sweeping over the harbour we could see the panoply of yachts and boats, large, small, and some enormous. It appeared that the yacht to which we were going was not in the harbour. There were also some pretty big vessels out in the outer harbour. It became clear that we were heading for one of the biggest, big enough to have its own heli-deck. We flicked round and hovered before slowly dropping in, directed by a deck hand with pink ping-pong bats. The rotors slowly stopped. We got out and I looked around. The deck was holystoned planking. All the deck fittings gleamed in the strong afternoon sun. There was an inevitable air of well being and rich pampered living. The whiteness of the super-structure was dazzling. The crewmen were all smartly dressed in white t-shirts and white jeans. It was like a commercial for the latest super wash soap powder. As we walked along the deckside gangway under the canopy I noticed that the vessel was flying a Cayman Islands flag. I had been involved at one time in registering a yacht and knew something about different registers and their flags. Towards the stern we turned down a short stairway of beautifully maintained mahogany. The escort tapped discreetly on a large solid door and then went in. I followed.

There were just two men in the large lounge cabin. Rosewood panelled walls. Elegant, very expensive tailor-made furniture. A Raoul Dufy, I'm sure, over a real marble mantelshelf. One of occupants was sitting behind a tidy desk. Hardly anything on it. He was not an especially distinguished looking man. In fact unobtrusive was a good description. Dark, greying, neatly trimmed hair. Asian looks but not obvious. Good blue-grey suit. But somehow he emanated power. One thing which struck me almost immediately was that he didn't seem to blink his eyes at all. They just stayed open. I think snakes are a bit like that.

The other person in the room was not unfamiliar to me. The hackles on my neck were rising. This was Blondie – the Russian Mafia hit-man who had been in 'Les Feuilles.' And very possibly the same guy as the one who bashed me during the kidnap. He wasn't looking my way, just looking out of the cabin window.

The escort said simply "Mr Piercy, sir." He gave a short head-bow and left the room. My host – I'd no idea of his name – looked at me impassively. I felt slightly pissed off by all this stuff and I thought I would take over.

"Well, Mr whoever you are, I'm here. I've got the contract. I've been assured that Gabriella Enders will be released once you have these papers. So here they are."

I opened the attaché case and put two plastic folders onto the table.

"There is one full set, copies; and the remainder of the

originals in the other folder." I pushed that folder over to him. "These plus the ones I gave to your – legal – representative make up a full set. They have all been signed by Mr Enders". I then gently slid the second file over to him. "I suggest you sign this copy-set for me to take back to Mr Enders."

He picked up the originals and began to read. I wondered if Gary was right about the clever clauses which would protect him in the future. How well buried are they? Will this guy spot them?. He had said nothing since I came in. He read carefully and quietly. When he had finished he opened a desk drawer took out the sheets I had given them earlier, made up the full set and slid them back into the desk. Then he took a thick black Mont Blanc fountain pen from his jacket and signed the copy set. He pushed them over to me and pressed a bell by the door. Then he sat back and looked at me. The escort came back into the lounge cabin. He indicated with his arm the doorway. I put the copy into my case. Then I leaned on the desk, quite close to the man sitting behind it.

"Gabriella better be released very soon." I said quietly. "Very soon."

I thought I saw a quick sparkle of anger in his eyes, then he turned away.

I was back in my hotel by 4.30. There were messages from Gary Enders and from the auto industry specialists I had contacted. I poured myself a large Ballantynes from the high-class drink fridge in the room. Then I called Gary. A nice brief, tight, conversation. He seemed relieved that this time the document hand-over had gone smoothly. I didn't say much. I would now await results.

"I've done my part, now I am waiting for news of Gabriella's release", I said. Gary assured me that he would now be able to organise this fairly soon.

I waited for a dramatic couple of minutes and then said. "Right, well now I hope you understand me. I've had enough of this for a game of soldiers. I want her out and I want me out."

I managed to catch the other callers before they finished their working day. I got some rather interesting news from the Brightwell Consulting contact. It was rumoured that a big Far-East group was offering a lot of money to take over one of the leading British teams and – even more interesting – the same buyer was interested in one of the leading UK race-engine design and build groups.

The actual buyer was obscure, well shielded by shell

companies; but the word was said that a Hong Kong holding company seemed to be involved. I didn't tell him why I wanted to know and he didn't press. We made the conventional agreement to meet for a drink when we were both in London. "I owe you one", I said almost convincingly mentally embarrassed by the social cliché.

The news from the professor at Coventry Poly was less specific but in its way more significant in the macro-sense. There was major restructuring being planned by at least two major Eastern manufacturing groups in the auto sector – with some serious financial backing – and on a scale which could only mean plans for dramatic expansion of markets. And these plans included massive investment in plants in new country locations in the East.

Chapter *9*

Our British motorsport party at the Paddock Club was in full swing when I arrived, looking a cool cat in my Cerruti cream linen jacket. A couple of glasses of Krug and I also felt the cool cat. In a sense it was my party but at this stage I had finished my main role. I had in effect handed in my exam paper. Nothing more I could do except circulate and push a few carefully chosen words into the right shell-like ears. After the second glass I stood on one side and viewed the action. This was a genuine high-life scene.

It must have been one of the highest concentrations of beautiful women you could find anywhere. Sleek blondes with long bronzed backs and perfectly fitting white dresses. Dark eyed beauties with black hair, wearing dramatic exciting flame red or jewel blue. And everywhere the flash and flesh of long shapely legs ...

I picked out a clutch of VIP's and celebrities. The Duke of Kent was chatting and laughing with a lively group: a couple of racing drivers who were almost certainly drinking mineral water and a representative group of lovely ladies or babes. The Ambassador was showing the French Minister of Sport the small exhibition of vintage British cars. We had an ERA, a BRM, a Vanwall, Le Mans Jaguar D type, Le Mans Bentley and a nice Frazer - Nash 2 litre from 1956.

The Princess had put in appearance representing local Royalty. She was with the President of the Monaco Automobile Club. He was showing her the enlarged photograph of William Grover Johnson, the Englishman who won the first ever Monaco Grand Prix in 1929. So a long British connection.

I must admit to feeling pretty self-satisfied. The right people were here. A big splash on the high level social scene at a competitive time and place. Press cameras had been flashing and I knew we should get some very good coverage. Just then I heard a whisper in my ear. The soft American voice.

"The limey's looking like the cat who got the cream. Miaaow." I turned to see the quirky smile of Holly Bright close up behind me.

"Hullo, trouble-maker" I said. "Thanks for all the in-put at the press party. Just exactly what I needed." She put her tongue out at me - a delicious little pink thing - and grinned.

"You really needed it" she said. "You looked far too smug, too well organised. I was just de-stuffing you."

" 'Stuffing' has a rather rude connotation in real English" I told her. She curved an eyebrow.

"Sounds fun. Anyway, are you done here?"

"Yep", I nodded. "All done and dusted."

"Right, then I am declaring an armistice. I am buying you dinner." She tucked her arm through mine. That's when I saw Kate. She was talking with a fawning gang of journalists and TV cameramen. The small wiry guy from French TV almost has his tongue hanging out as he was looking at her. Can't think what he had in mind. Almost immediately she spotted me. I must have sent out some waves which she picked up. Charmingly but brutally she disengaged from the journalists and sauntered over towards us. When she was just about in talking distance, and ignoring Holly, she spoke in the poteen flavoured voice - smooth but with a hell of a kick. "Well hello, lover boy: and how's the big man doing tonight." There was enough innuendo in the comment but she piled on the pressure by letting her hand rest on my shoulder while planting a soft kiss, not on my cheek, but on my mouth. Still she completely disregarded Holly. I moved in to salvage something.

"Holly, this is Kate O'Malley, PR Director of the O'Horan Team. And this is Holly Bright, an American journalist." Now Kate turned very slowly towards Holly with a very cool appraising look. She was taller than the petite Holly and she used this advantage rather destructively to dominate the scene. She still rested her hand on my shoulder.

"Hello", she said to Holly, not offering a handshake. "I'm sure you are finding Formula One much more exciting than - what is it, Champ Cars - in the States?" Holly disengaged her arm from mine.

"Oh, you are so right", she said in a very exaggerated Southern belle accent. "It's too, too much for a little old Kentucky girl like me." She glanced at me and cocked a beautifully arched eyebrow. "Somehow", she said, "I have the funniest feeling that we aren't going to dinner together tonight. See you sometime."

She nodded at Kate and moved away. As far as I could judge she was heading for the exit door. I felt a twinge of something. But before it could have much effect Kate said,

"Well Mister Piercy, I must say that you do get around. Just as well I'm here to protect you from all these, scheming females." Her smile and her light touch on my shoulder stirred memories of our night together. The long, knowing fingers and bright green nails renewed promises of pleasure. I surrendered.

"Hello Kate", I said somewhat hoarsely. "It's good to see you. Really good I mean. Let's get out of here. Your place or mine?" She looked at me with a cat like smile which seemed to engulf me.

"Whoa, boy" she said. "You're moving too fast there. Revving too hard. I've got a dinner date tonight - business you know." I felt my heart do a familiar lurch of disappointment. I tried to keep up the debonair style.

"Ok, tomorrow?" I knew the saintly smile was a bit feeble and lopsided. So did she.

"It's such a busy week", she sighed over-acting. "But maybe I'll catch up with you in London." She turned away and I saw her signal to a well known TV personality in the international motor racing world. Another bastard, lucky bastard actually, who just seemed to go from strength to strength. And with a dangerous reputation where women were concerned. What did they see in him apart from his fantastic looks, excellent physique, exciting life style and pots of money? Ok so it's my party and I'll cry if I want to.

To say I felt let down would be a total understatement. I felt gutted or as contemporary sportsmen are prone to say 'Gu-edd.' Whatever happened to the glottal stop? Why had she come on while Holly was there, then left me in the lurch. Some sort of sadistic pleasure? Or was I being paranoid? Even if a woman doesn't want a man at a particular moment she likes to keep him on a string. I grinned at myself: I'd been a bit of a chump to think that this virtual super-model could have any interest on me. I'm a nice guy but nothing special. I finished another champagne cocktail and silently slipped away. Considering my starring role I felt that my exit caused less than a rush of excitement. Nobody noticed. I was becoming paranoid about my memorable non-exits.

Out on the harbour round, I looked for a taxi. Plenty of them but all apparently engaged. I wish taxis around the world would have a standard signal system to tell you whether they're available. I walked in the direction of the hotel pausing each minute or so to see if a cab was coming. Suddenly as I passed a darkish entrance a large figure stepped out. It was the white-blond Russian from the café. I didn't like this one little bit. He seemed to be alone but it was scant comfort. I saw a couple of people coming along but somehow they scented trouble and like most of us crossed to the other side of the road. The Samaritan parable seems to have found few converts over the centuries.

"Mr Piercy", he said in decent but strongly accented English: "I am not happy with the way you behaved last time we met. Tonight you don't have your football team and I am alone. Just the two of us. I am a professional and you hurt my pride. Now I am going to hurt you. Not seriously but enough to make you remember me. Lets say you will not be giving pleasure to your lady friends for some time. And - this is personal. Just from me – Viktor."

He moved towards me looking as menacing as a pit bull. Years ago as a black belt in the Tiger Judo Club I had made friends with an old Japanese Judokwai. He had helped me to prepare for my black belt first grading: he was very much of the old school and had strong views about the honourable behaviour of Judo practitioners. He had taught me a special move - quite different and unorthodox. But it was extremely dangerous and he made me swear that I would never use it unless it was in self defence. In my book Viktor was as good a paid-up representative of the forces of evil as I was ever likely to encounter. I had not done my Judo for years and I had never used the move in anger. Sometimes things do go right and this did. To his complete surprise I moved right into him and stabbed my fingers into his neck. The angle, the speed, the balance were just perfect. He went straight down. I did not stay to check his state of health. If he was alive I was sensitive to the fact that he would be a tad angry; if he was dead I didn't want to be around when the police arrived. Quickly I crossed the road into a more public well-lit area and continuing my short run of luck I found a cab at once.

Back in my room the shock affect hit me. No guilt. Quite a bit of fear. And maybe a sneaking bit of male pride.

Anyway I slept well and was up bright and early for the race. My run of luck continued. My promotion activities also went well. No hitches, glitches. All the world's cameras seemed to be focused on the Prince when the world champion drove him round in a Jaguar XK8. The parade of British racing green greats looking stunning. Damien Miller drove a famous American film star round the circuit and afterwards she stood on the podium and told the audience - and world TV - that English cars are the best: very pretty and very fast. Great stuff.

The race was something of a disappointment for me personally though. There was a pile up at the start which took out three of the front two rows. My protege Jonathan managed to avoid the meleé and was running a strong second. After about twenty laps it seemed clear that Jonathan's "Low-Wear" hard compound tyres were holding up better than Willi Schwarzkopf - who was running a softer version. Excitement was mounting in the Brit camp as the Johnson Racing crept closer to the scarlet leader. Jonathan was braking later and carrying more speed through the quicker corners with his stronger tyres. But passing at Monaco is a black art. Most experts reckon that it can't be done unless there is a real differential between the cars or driver skills. We were beginning to think in terms of settling for a pretty good podium place when three things happened. The Italian car slowed going into the tunnel; Jonathan drew level to pass; the offside rear tyre on the other car blew and disintegrated throwing it out of control and into the Johnson car. They were both out and beyond repair. The good news was that neither was hurt. The red flags were out and the British course car led them all round until the tunnel was cleared. The race was eventually won by Donald Coltherne who seems to go well at Monaco. So that was pretty good for British prestige.

They discovered afterwards that the Scuderia Fratelli had

collected a small piece of errant debris from the start pile-up and this had eventually punctured the tyre.

The formal dinner at Monaco is always a very grand occasion - by far the poshest of them all. You have to pack your DJ. So there I was again putting on the style, this time in a natty little number from Huntsman - one of Savile Row's finest. Sumptuous is the word that comes to mind to describe the sheer luxury and over-the-top glamour of the occasion and the setting. A kaleidoscope of rich colour - gold somehow predominantly - and the brilliance of the fine jewellery, much of it in rather large lumps. You had to ask yourself 'What is it all about?' Rather stupid facile images of the starving in Africa create the odd twinge of remorse but it is all to easily assuaged by the thought that all this is creating work, jobs. A glass or two of champagne and you begin to feel that this is charity work.

I did my bit again: nodding, smiling, pressing palms, clapping arms round shoulders in a manly way. But I wearied rather more quickly than usual. Gabriella was still a captive. I had heard nothing about her release although Gary has assured me that it was imminent. Just stay cool. I thought I would get back to London fairly quickly. I felt that I would be better able to do something there if necessary. It would also give me the opportunity to put some pressure on Gary.

An early start back next day would mean a pretty clear head tonight. Once again I felt like Cinderella leaving the party. I just wasn't in the mood. My mood was given another injection of gloom when I saw Kate dancing cosily with the boyo from the previous night; and shortly afterwards I spotted Holly Bright chatting animatedly, eyes living up to her name, with a couple of Italian drivers. They obviously found her very attractive. I hadn't actually looked at her as a babe but I could now see just how attractive she was. I turned away feeling unjustifiably bitter. I carried away the feeling that she may have seen me out of the corner of her eye. I let the top-hatted doorman do his stuff this time and snaffle a taxi for me. A good fifty francs value I reckoned as I arrived safely at my hotel. I packed my stuff and generally got things sorted out ready for next morning. I called down to have the bill prepared. Once again the bed felt cool and crisp, very refreshing. I lay within the sheets and luxuriated for a time in sheer sybaritic pleasure.

But I began to think about things. My usual compulsion in this situation. What did I really feel for Kate O'Malley? Had it just been a one-night-stand? Fantastic sex but nothing more.

Perhaps a better question was what does she feel for me? Did we have any future? I knew I was being a bit naive. But the thought was there so I had to admit it. No answers presented themselves and I moved on. What about Gabby? She seemed nicer than she had before. Perhaps life with Gary had knocked something out of her. She said it was all over between them. I realised that I still felt something special for her because of my real concern and anger at Gary for his cavalier attitude. As I began to speculate on the possibility of re-kindling our relationship I fell asleep. I think that was significant: it felt good and I drifted comfortably into sleep.

The journey home was uneventful. No black windowed Mercedes pursuing me and shoving me off the road. Yes I had actually considered the possibly. I drove straight through with just statutory three-hour breaks for coffee and croissants and the odd 30-minute nap. The beauty of the Channel tunnel is that another train really does come along quite soon and not long after reaching the port I was boarded and on the way.

In London I was in a strange mood. A feeling of animated suspense. Everything was working at a distance, dispassionate and disconnected. Life went on but somehow it had nothing to do with me. Perhaps I didn't want the reality to intrude until

Gabby was safe.

Back at the Mews flat I flicked through my post and, finding not much of interest, stuck it on the silver galley tray to deal with later, if ever. Half a grapefruit and a bowl of porridge later I was driving into the office. A bit anti-social really using the car in London but I do need it available to get quickly to Silverstone – or so I tell myself.

Carolyn came in half an hour after me - and still twenty-five minutes before she was due. She seemed really pleased to see me. "How did it go?" She asked with genuine enthusiasm. "I've seen several pictures and I've taped a couple of broadcasts. It did seem to work didn't it?" I gave her a quick review of events her over a cup of tea. English strong breakfast brew. She brought in a copy of 'Autosport' – the top motorsport publication in the world – to show me their full report on our British promotion.

I started to look at the schedule for our campaign and realised that I now had to focus my next effort on the forth-coming event in Ireland, Dublin in fact. I was really looking forward to this. I had always loved Ireland, having lived there for a while. This was a typical Irish situation. It was not a real Grand Prix but in its own way it was going to be a hell of a party and unique. That great character Frank O'Horan had got the idea of taking F1 cars to Ireland. He felt as an Irishman that they were entitled to see the real thing in action. It was handy enough that some top drivers lived just outside Dublin. The new popular President - although pretty disinterested in motor racing - saw the promotional benefit and was working with Frank to make it happen. Another very big hitter, a local boy who had made good – very good – in the world of international finance - was coming in with some serious sponsorship. It was going to take place in Phoenix Park almost in the centre of Dublin and the idea was to create some of the retro atmosphere of the thirties when racing was held there. There had been a few late meetings in the fifties as well; handicap races which the Irish used to like, perhaps a horse-racing heritage. They were hoping that Scuderia Fratelli would send a car and I had persuaded Johnson Racing to provide a car for Jonathan.

It was really intended to be more of an exhibition than a race but when you put racers into exciting machinery they are likely to be heavy booted on the throttle pedal. So it was going to be fun. There would also be some real parties - not the Monaco floss. A well-organised drinking programme to train for the few days in Dublin was advisable. I had arranged the Jaguar course car again and British motor heritage success demonstrations.

I reminisced about "Dublin Days." The back bar in Jammets: tacky if anyone ever looked at it in detail but with so much style, character and such great seafood that you never needed to look in detail. I remembered having my first black-velvet there in a silver half pint tankard one Christmas Eve. The cranks who say it's a waste to spoil good champagne by mixing it with Guinness lack the imagination of a gnat. Fizz and the black stuff are horse and carriage together. Well it would be interesting to go back and check out the old sod, although Jammets, the Russell, Hibernian and the Dolphin were long since gone.

The paper work for Dublin was OK. Carolyn was very reliable. But now she seemed to be popping in and out of my office like a yo-yo. Finally she told me "Dan, I have to leave."

"OK" I said, "just go when you are ready."

"No" she blurted out; "I mean resign. Tony has been promoted to a job in Paris and we have to move soon."

I leaned back in my chair and regarded her.

"Heh", I said "I'm sorry for me; but I'm pleased for you and Tony." I walked round the desk and gave her a hug and a kiss on the cheek.

"Paris is a beautiful city", I said "you'll love it." I went back behind the desk and sat down. We talked dates and details. Then I said,

"OK let's have a celebration drink."

We left the office together.

As we went out from the building and crossed to a favourite haunt of mine from way back just up from the Scotch house, I happened to notice a car parked just by the barracks, illegally of course. I say happened to notice but in fact I had been twitchy and on the qui vive ever since I got back. I think the car had the distinctive Monaco plates – but that didn't make much sense.

Carolyn and I had a rather boozey slushy sentimental hour. Then I put her in a taxi and took a taxi myself. Too much drink taken to drive.

Back in the mews house I couldn't decide whether to go for a meal or make myself something at home. I didn't much feel staying in – the place felt damned lonely and the farewell drink's session hadn't helped my mood. On the other hand eating-out, alone, wasn't an appetising thought either. In the end I caved in to watch a film on TV, a light hearted romantic comedy with a decidedly happy ending. I watched it while scoffing a home-made burger, smothered in onions. I had one or two important things to do next day before leaving for Dublin that evening. So an early night was in order. I decided against any more alcohol and settled for a large Horlicks –not a word to my drinking companions on the F1 scene. It helped but I was still a long time getting to sleep. Too many images, too many issues.

Chapter *10*

My first call next day was to my financial adviser at one of the smaller merchant banks. He specialised in looking after personal portfolios and although mine was titchey by their standards he took me on because of our long standing friendship. He was I suppose family; a sort of distant second cousin. But more importantly we had been friends at school. I haven't always kept up with many school friends but this one had stuck. We could just pick it up whenever we met.

I arranged to see him at his City office mid morning and trying to make allowances for the traffic round Bank meant that in the end I was early. I quite enjoyed sitting in the large ground floor reception area, polished granite floors with lots of glass and light. Outside was a broad piazza with steady streams of people passing by or crossing it.

I began to notice an interesting phenomenon. I calculated that eighty percent of the women wore skirts with heeled shoes. Some high heels, some medium heels, a few ultra-high. I reckon about half the skirts were short, even very short. The other half were long - even ankle length.

In the west end it was pretty much the reverse. Most of the ladies were in trousers, ranging from jeans to smart suit trousers.

I pondered on why this might be. Is it that the City, all banks, lawyers and solid institutions, is that much more traditional. Do bankers like their neatly skirted secretaries to perch note-book in hand to take dictation. I think not, but perhaps tradition does hold some sway.

The West End - female PR execs, designers, fashion marketers - is perhaps more emancipated. Still it's a bit strange. Ah well.

As I sat there in the pleasant morning light and comfortable lounger I did a quick reversal of thought. I didn't want to apply my intellectual effort only to topics relating to female legs and dress-codes. Far from it. You would often catch me making forecasts about the future of the world, the prospects for mankind. Can we possibly avoid total unemployment by 2050? When will computers finally take over? How soon before we discover life on other stars and begin galactical colonisation? Shouldn't we begin soon to educate people for living - assuming they'll never have a job - and forget the work ethic? How are we going to avoid massive social disaffection within countries and between countries? But I can't get worked up about the threat of a perforated ozone belt.

All good stuff. I was about to branch into prophecies of a legless society interned within high security dwellings when a pleasant faced, medium length skirted, young lady approached me.

"The reception desk told me that you are Mr Piercy. Mr Sikorski is ready now; would you like to come with me please? I'll see you through security."

She took me up to Peter's office. He came, smiling, to meet me. His father was Polish and Peter had inherited some of the crazy brilliance that many of that nationality seem to have.

"Dan," he said "It's been too long. Let's sit down over here."

We went to a small sofa and table with the statutory coffee pot, cups and an assortment of expensive biscuits. I took one. Then another while we chatted and sipped coffee.

I explained to him that I had got a thing about investing in one of two of the up and coming firms involved in the internet, e-commerce and websites. I didn't know much about the sector technically or even commercially but I had a feeling and I wanted to get in. Investments which could bring very big bucks with flotation. "But not too risky," I told him.

"Ah," he retorted "There's the rub."

We worked out how much I could afford to flutter with and he promised to make some enquiries and let me have some proposals when I got back from Dublin. At the back of my mind I was half-ready to say something about my situation. It was really why I had called on him: the investment idea was real but could easily have waited. But something he said then pre-empted me.

"Have you heard from Gabriella recently," he asked. He knew, of course, all about our divorce. In fact I know that he had also been advising Gabriella quite independent of me about her financial affairs. I'd introduced them way back.

"I had a letter the other day," I said.

"Yes, well, I think she and Gary are splitting," Peter said reflectively. "She's been sounding me out about her current financial status and I got the impression she's also been talking to a lawyer."

I still didn't know quite how to handle things, how much to

say. Peter became aware of my unease.

"What's wrong," he asked, "You're not going to be a bloody fool and take her back are you?" I felt I had to say something.

"Peter, it isn't that but I think she is in some danger and I'm trying to help. It's tied up in some way with Gary's business."

"He always was a tricky bastard," chipped in Peter. "I wouldn't trust the sod with the milk money."

"Yes, and I've got to admit that I think you are right. He fooled me for a long time in more ways than one."

We looked at each other for a couple of minutes, his pale eyes questioning.

"Look, the real reason I came to see you is to ask you to take good care of this package. If anything should happen to me - oh it's a very small chance believe me - please open it and take whatever action is necessary."

He nodded. "Of course. But don't you want to tell me something more about it now? Perhaps I could help?"

I shook my head decisively. "No, I'd rather not get you involved. If you could just keep these papers really safe that would be great. I'd better tell you that someone may be after them."

"OK, I'll stick 'em in our bloody vault - safe as the Bank of England down there."

He arranged it while I was there and I must say it made me feel a sight easier.

As I left the bank by taxi I kept a look out but couldn't see any suspicious characters. The taxi driver seemed amused by my somewhat furtive glances. I think he reckoned I was being pursued by an angry husband. Because of the possibility of that impure thought I sanctioned him with a tip fifty percent of my normal. That would fix him.

I had decided to drop in at the 'Gear Knob' club, a hideaway for motoring scribes, minor team officials, lower rank drivers and sundry hangers on. Kate O'Mally was still very much in my thoughts - and not just lustfully. She was a bit of an intriguing mystery woman. I did want to know her better. We seemed to hit if off. So some gentle research might do no harm.

Toby Batchum was sitting at the bar and I took a hard wooden stool alongside.

"By God," he said touching his forelock, "it's his Ambassadorship come to hob-nob with the likes of us." He grinned and stuck out a hand.

"What are you having, Dan?"

After a patter a small talk and a few draughts of best bitter I raised the subject of Kate O'Mally - rather diplomatically I thought. I knew that he was one of the journalists who was really in with the teams, including Jordan. The diplomacy though was not enormously successful.

"Aha, you're another one after that, are you? Well join the club and the queue. It's a very long one though". Then he spoke rather seriously.

"No, she's a good kid and very good at her job, highly professional. She comes on with the ultra-sophisticated dame bit and she's got a tongue like an open razor, cut you into ribbons; but underneath it she's nice. I've seen her being really kind to some new youngsters in the business - but only when she thinks no one is looking; she wants to keep her hard-nosed reputation."

That was interesting because Toby had been around and he was, in my book, an excellent judge of character.

"What's her background. Do you know?" I asked.

"Well she was apparently in the States for a number of

years promoting an Irish pop-band. I've an idea one of her brothers, or cousin maybe, was the lead singer. She got involved with the O'Horan team because the band is one of its sponsors and she started by looking after their involvement in the team. It sort of developed from that. So where did you meet her and what's the interest? - as if I need to ask."

I gave him a quick round-up and said quite openly that I liked her and hoped to get to meet her again soon. Somehow we had kept missing one another.

"Does she ever come in here?" I asked.

"Never seen her. Don't think this rough-trade is quite her scene, though."

"Do you happen to know whether she has a bloke?" I slipped the question in. He gave me a slightly quizzical look.

"I'd say you're a tad smitten," he said. "But the answer is I don't know, but no - I don't think so. Not from what I've heard any way. Quite a few chaps asking about her but the consensus is that she is very much committed to career at present. Rather a determined lady in that regard. So the field is pretty clear, I'd say."

I bought another round and we chatted about the season. He upset me a bit by asking whether I thought Jonathan Piery would stay with Johnson Racing. I told him very definitely yes and asked why he thought otherwise. He shrugged.

"You know how it is in this business. Always chopping and changing. And at this stage in the year people start speculating on driver and team changes. But in fact there have been some pretty strong rumours that Jonathan has been talking seriously elsewhere."

"Well he really is settled at Johnson," I assured him, "we talked about it at Monaco. I think Johnson will make a confirmatory announcement quite soon. In fact you could pip your journalist competitors by making a positive statement in the next issue." I hoped he would. It might help Jonathan.

I left Toby, pint in front of him, fag in mouth burning away brightly. And, I was glad to see his notebook in hand while he pencilled in something or other. I hoped it was to the effect that Jonathan was firm at Johnson.

I'd already left my bags in the office and I called in en route to the airport. There was a chauffeur limo waiting to take me out to Heathrow where I would fly to Dublin care of Aer Lingus. I grabbed my bags and documentation, all beautifully organised by Carolyn and gave her a peck on the cheek.

"See you next Monday, Miss Money Penny," I said. "No

slipping off to Paris before I'm back."

She waved me out with a touch of a sad smile I think. Probably my imagination, though.

Chapter 11

Dublin had changed. The run in from the airport used to go through some sixties, rather brash, housing estates dominated by large modern churches. As you came into the city centre, the scene became a collection of old dingy looking bars with names like Mooneys, Egans select snug and even Finnegans. Although they looked scruffy they had character. Now the mini-motorway passed through modern slick industrial estates with high tech companies assembling computers. And the pubs had been beautified with EU money. All very proper: improving tourist facilities as part of Ireland's economic development. Progress is progress; but the old Dublin was a lot of fun. Perhaps I would find out what the new version had to offer.

I had flown in to pick up a car here. It used to be messy to bring one by sea to Ireland. Once again Rover had fixed me up with a little MG this time in a rather fetching shade of metallic puce. Not my personal colour choice but it's a great little mover and I enjoyed the drive. They seemed to have done a little work on the engine - a VVC. It was very peppy.

I was staying at the Shelbourne on Stephens's Green; surely one of the great hotels. It certainly was in my time in Dublin. They used to have a blackboard at the porter's desk. If there was a message or telephone call for a VIP - that is someone who spent a lot of time drinking in the Horseshoe bar - a bell boy would go round the various rooms holding up the board with a name chalked on it and ringing a school-bell. It frightened a lot of people on occasions and often woke up a few post lunch drinkers. An acquaintance of mine, an impoverished Anglo-Irish peer frequently had his name displayed. I was delighted to find that there was the same cheerful, almost homely, service and I was soon comfortably installed.

Apart from the arrangements at the racing circuit I had to deal with a couple of things - see a few people, one in particular. A personal matter you might say.

Before I left London, Gary had telephoned me at my Office. I was rather surprised because I had got the impression that he wanted to keep our conversations secret, well away from the official scene. He had promised to let me know what had been agreed with the syndicate about Gabriella's release but I had expected him to set-up a lunch or drinks meeting somewhere unobtrusive. In fact when he called me he spoke very openly. The syndicate had verified the documents and they were satisfied that the contract was legal and binding. I wondered about the small escape clause traps which Gary said had been built in. But I didn't ask. The hell with Gary and his contract: what I wanted was Gabriella out of it, fast.

It was Wednesday. The Phoenix Park meeting was starting on Friday. On Thursday it was the key day, according to Gary Enders when Gabby would be released. My feelings about her were in a real mess. I obviously found her very attractive sexually; I was clearly still very fond of her. But I had strong reservations about her ethics. I knew she was very selfish and a pretty hard bitten character. I didn't really admire her ... but she had a way of drawing me into a relationship, despite myself. Oh well, the first thing is to get her out of the present danger. Then we would see. As you get older I think you develop a more fatalistic approach to life. Hell pretty much everything you have tried to plan up until now has proved irrelevant. The real pattern of your life has very little to do with you. Just roll with the punches.

I thought a jar or two would do no harm so I went to the bar and renewed acquaintance with Powers Gold Label. I was sipping it quietly when they paged me to take a telephone call.

Gary Enders had set-up a meeting just outside Dublin, early on Thursday morning, at a well-known pub and restaurant called the Lamb Doyles. In the old days it was a late-night drinking place where bona fide travellers - people who had driven five miles out of central Dublin could go on drinking. The Lamb Doyles was just next to its huge car park and the rendezvous was to be there at 8.00am when it would be deserted. Gabriella would be left there for me to pick her up. The deal made by Gary with the mysterious syndicate was no police, no follow-up. Everything just back to normal. Whatever that might be in these complicated times. My idea of normal had certainly undergone some drastic revision over the past few weeks. I cant' say I was very happy about the arrangement. Why couldn't they just release her in Dublin? Put her in a taxi to the Shelbourne? Gary had said that there was a strong wish for them to keep out of any sort of involvement. And also a bit of power play, keeping control.

I used my mobile to call a number at an address near Chapelizod past the Park on the way out of Dublin. Rosie was a very good friend. I was probably in love with her at one time; but things conspired against us later. she married a successful Irish businessman - a nice guy - and had a Catholic sized family. I hadn't seen her for a while but we had kept in touch. We used to have something special and I sometimes wondered what might have been. Through her family - not her husband's - she had some good connections. I thought it wouldn't do any harm to talk with her. She was at home. We laughed and teased each other a bit.

"Mary Mother of Jesus, where have you come from? Ruined my life you did." Big giggle. "Oh my God. I suppose I'll have to meet you. Will I recognise you? I expect time and other things have taken a toll."

I suggested meeting at a famous bar in Duke Street, but she told me it had been pulled down. So we arranged to meet in the Shelbourne bar.

She was as blonde and pretty as ever despite her forty plus years. Big grey eyes, retroussé nose, slightly pouting lips and great legs. Completely different from that other Irish woman of my recent acquaintance, Kate O'Malley, in looks and personality. Rosie was a bit of a softie. Rather like me.

"Still leading the good life I see" she said with a well-remembered twinkle, "always the smart dresser. I daresay that jacket cost a few hundred."

It was really good the way we slipped so quickly into an easy intimacy. The years melted away. She wouldn't let me kiss her when we met.

"Ah, I know where your kisses lead" she said as she sat down tucking her nice knees together and throwing me the impish grin. But she put her hand on my arm lightly, and it felt good. We caught up on the recent past. She was obviously intrigued by my divorce.

"I'm not surprised she left you - she probably was overwhelmed by your sexual demands" Rosie said lightly but with a touch of underlying satisfaction. Then I told her about the current scene and the present real-life problem of Gabriella's kidnap. I told her virtually everything. There were three reasons for this. I trusted her absolutely. I wanted her help with a contact, some back up. And she was some insurance: if anything happened to me she knew the background. I explained this to her. She grasped it quickly but was obviously frightened as hell. She couldn't believe that this sort of stuff was happening to me - an ordinary guy - and people I knew.

"Dan", she said squeezing my arm tightly now, "you must go to the Garda Siochana, the police. These are really dangerous people, and this isn't Moscow, it's Ireland."

Then she stopped suddenly. Ireland was no stranger to bloody violence, to kidnapping, to gangs of assassins. I knew what she was thinking.

"Do you ever hear from Liam?" I asked quietly. He was a second cousin or some distant relative who owned a stud in County Kildare, the blue-grass County of Ireland. I had known him very well at one time, a long time ago. He had been a high up in the IRA then in charge of a territory, after a period as one of the most feared field operatives the organisation had. But like a number of the early IRA members he was an idealist - a patriotic freedom fighter - and when the strategy moved from war against the British Army to civilian terror attacks, Liam opted out. It was testimony to his reputation that the IRA leaders accepted this. The legend is that it is very difficult to retire from the IRA, alive. Since then he had simply been running quietly, but quite successfully, his small farm and stud.

I had helped him once - saved his life I suppose - in a way. At the time he had been out of the IRA organisation for a year or so but was still on the British suspect list. It happened when he was in a difficult spot, almost caught by a platoon of Paras in a Belfast bar. I knew from Rosie about his background and that he had severed all connections with the IRA. He had been a gunman but he had never used bombs or acted against civilians. In fact, he had never assassinated anyone - not even military targets. But he had fought some battles with British troops. I had met him a few times since his retirement and despite his history I liked him as a man. And it was difficult to condemn his motives - as he saw them - as a freedom fighter. There was also a deep personal motivation: his ten year old bother had been killed by a stray British plastic bullet during a panic reaction to an emergency when the troops fired at militant civilians who were demonstrating over-zealously. Plastic bullets are intended not to do serious injury but by terrible chance it hit the child on the temple. This was just one more death in a stupid vicious war but Rosie was convinced that it pushed a quite studious young man into violence.

My mind flash-backed to the time when I intervened in the incident with the Paras.

I was just finishing a drink in the Central bar in Belfast when I saw him come in looking behind him through the door. I'd been in Belfast talking to an up and coming Ulster F3 driver and had made a nostalgic return to my haunts. Liam bought a Bushmills and sat down. He hadn't see me then. Suddenly the Paras came in, three of them led by a baby faced officer. They looked round the room in what was a typical pattern at that time. Without thinking I went and sat down at Liam's table.

"Liam, old boy", I said loudly in my best hooting upper class British accent. "How are you, dear feller? How's Rosie?" He picked up the message fast.

"Dan, hello, it's good to see you again. When was the last time - at the Wasps club bar, wasn't it?" We dropped into comfortable reminiscence about rugby and racing. Very clubby, U style conversation. Then I made a meal of recognising the Paras. I had been one and even now I was a card carrying ex-regimental officer. I stood up and walked over to the young Officer, glass in my hand.

"Evening, Lieutenant", I said briskly putting out my free hand. He looked at me, some uncertainty in his eyes. I smiled and said easily,

"Sorry if I'm a bit familiar but you're from my old regiment. Retired now. But I keep in touch. D'you know Major Redding?" I knew George Redding was still in Ulster. He knew the Major and I asked him to pass on my regards. He probably wondered what I was doing in the bar. But a lot of British officers had assignments in civilian clothes and I could have been on a special mission. We chatted a moment. Then I went back to sit with Liam.

The Paras stayed a couple of minutes longer, looked round - not very seriously - and moved out, the Officer raising his hand to his beret in my direction as he went through the door. That incident founded a strange bond between Liam and me and I know that it would always be there.

Rosie answered my question, bringing me back to the present.

"Liam does keep in touch", she said. "He's making a great go of the stud, got some great horses going through. One or two of their two year olds have been doing well." She paused. "But he had a bad time in his personal life. He never had much time for women in the old days. On the run. Ducking and diving. We heard he'd met this woman about a year ago. Seems he really went in at the deep-end. We talked about it - he was so happy - so warm - but he never introduced us. He said he wanted to be sure, didn't want to blow it. Then he invited us over for a weekend to meet her. They were going to get married. We were really pleased for him." She paused.

"Then just before we were due to meet her we got a shock message from him: it was all off. It came out later that she had left him cold - gone off with some other guy. And she had used Liam, just taken him for a lot of money. It hit him very hard. He's become a recluse, really."

"Rosie" I spoke seriously. "I want to see him, I need some help with this business. I don't want to tell you what I want - the last thing is to get you involved. But I must see Liam. Could you arrange it, please?" Rosie didn't hesitate.

"I'll be back" she said, getting up from the leather banquette seat by the wall of the bar. I rose too, old world courtesy dies hard although young women find it hilarious and irritating.

She was back in ten minutes.

"You can see him this afternoon" she said. "and he's only seeing you because it's you. Tread softly, he's badly bruised."

"Tread softly because you tread on my dreams." I, rather pompous really quoted Yeats. "Don't worry I've been there when Gabriella left me."

"But you are risking so much to help her now?" she reported quickly.

"Yes, and don't even think of asking me why."

She smiled softly and possibly blinked a tear. "I know why. It's because you're a lovely man. I loved you very much you know." With a toss of the head and a quirky smile she tossed away the maudlin mood. "Let's have another old jar." She waved to the white-jacketed barman. "I'm buying."

We didn't go up to my room. We didn't go to bed. Which was sad from my point of view. But somehow what we had between us was stronger than my sexual imperatives, which is saying a helluva lot. But the beauty of the farewell kiss had the quality of an orgasm. It stroked the soul. I knew that Rosie was more deeply embedded in my highly sentimental psyche than I had ever admitted to myself.

I collected the MG from the R.I.A.C. garage and reminded myself of the route out of the city to County Kildare. I knew that there had been a lot of changes, one-way systems, dual carriageway roads, since I had last driven out on the road to Kildare. But Dublin is a smallish compact city so there were no real problems even for a navigation duffer like me. The archetypal Irishman looking after the garage – with a well seasoned face and bushy ginger eyebrows – put me right for the first key moves after getting onto Dawson Street. Mick –

his name of course – didn't quite tell me that if he had been going where I wanted to go he wouldn't have started from here. But I think it was in his mind. I shook his hand and slipped him a couple of Euros.

As I drove round the square in the late afternoon sunshine, I enjoyed the nostalgia of Georgian terraces and the old-world style of St Stephens Green. It's interesting how - when submerged in troubles - we relish so much a few seconds of simple satisfaction.

Swinging the little car through the long sweeping curves of the Curragh - the home of the Irish Derby - gave me almost a sensual pleasure. Wonderful open country, with wide green verges and the race-course in the middle distance you can taste the clean fresh air. It was always a highlight on the way to Cork. There is a surrealistic quality about it: too good to be true. Funny how odd images come up on the mind-screen. The green, green, grass of home and all that. This was where the Irish breed and feed their wonderful race-horses.

Just outside Naas I turned onto a narrow side road. A couple of miles on, I turned again onto an even narrower road - the surface a touch rough and stony with tall hedges and trees.. Rosie's directions had been very clear. A mile along I saw the open iron gates, nothing grand, which led into the gravel drive. The grounds were spacious and neat - well maintained. Liam was that sort of man. High standards. The house was a nicely proportioned Georgian - not too big. I could see the stables and stud wing, a separate small complex backing on to a paddock and fields in which a few nice horses were grazing quietly. It was quite an elegant scene with the tangy chestnut colour of some of the horses showing as bright highlights against the soft green countryside. I drew up in front of the house and parked alongside a spanking new Range Rover and a field green well-worked Land Rover. The smart carriage and the dutiful work-horse side by side. I went up the steps to the balustrade outside the main door. The bell chimed deep inside the house, echoing into the hallway. When it opened I would not have been amazed to find some crone asking my business with a ruthless smirk. The woman who greeted me was in fact a sensible looking mid forties, nicely turned out in an old style maid's outfit.

"Good afternoon, sir" she said. "I daresay you would be Mr Piercy. Mr Sullivan will be over in a minute from the stables. He's asked me to show you into the drawing room. I've put some tea in there. You may fancy a cup while you're waiting."

She led the way through a small hall and into a large room with classic Georgian windows looking out onto fields sloping gently down to a fair sized lake. As I watched a flight of grey geese drifted through a gap in small copse of elms. Nothing wrong with the view. I poured myself a cup of tea, took a slice of home-made cake and looked round the room. A nice room. Some good bits of furniture which looked as old as the house - late eighteenth century. One or two pictures though I didn't recognise the artists. The pastoral watercolour was very appealing. There was one anomalous modern painting which despite its amazing bright colours and shapes somehow fitted in very well. I've always felt that really nice things, well designed, good quality, can always go together regardless of period and style.

I heard him coming into the room and turned. Physically he hadn't changed. In his cords and check flannelled shirt he looked compact and purposeful. Medium height, muscular. And somehow he always looked well balanced – on his toes so to speak, but relaxed. But his grey eyes now had a glazed appearance. In his thirty-nine years he had lived on a saw-tooth edge of pain, fear, anger and aggression. And now it seemed his failed love had broken his heart. He smiled, though, with genuine friendship as we shook hands. He slapped his arm over my shoulder.

"It's good to see you, Dan. A real surprise when Rosie called but a good one. Drink?"

"Well, I'm just after having a cup of tay." I said in my best stage - Irish. He grimaced.

"I'd say we need a proper drink." He poured a couple of large Powers. This was mildly unusual: he wasn't a hard drinker in the past, quite the opposite. It sent a signal that he was perhaps coping with his sad love life through the medium of the bottle.

"So why have you come to lovely County Kildare?" he asked. Rosie had obviously pushed the fact that my visit was for special reason.

"I want a gun" I said. He cocked a well-shaped black eyebrow.

"Now, you know, I don't think I quite heard you".

"Let's sit down" I said wearily. "I think I'd better tell you a story."

As with Rosie I told him pretty well everything. Even about the way Gabby left me for Gary. Actually I thought that might help him with his own problem. He leaned back.

"Well now, and isn't that the very devil", he said in his soft understated tone. "So you want a gun for a bit of protection; or are you planning on shooting your way in to do a rescue?"

"No way", I told him emphatically. "I just want to pick up Gabriella as agreed and deliver her safely back to London - or whatever she thinks is safest. We've got to do something about that – but first she has to be free. But each time I've met these people I get the feeling that it could turn nasty. The blond Russian, Viktor, has certainly got it in for me now, I'd just feel a bit more capable of defending myself if I was armed." He nodded slowly. He got up and raised his hand slightly.

"Wait."

He was gone about ten minutes and then he returned with a small parcel. He took out a rather small pistol - a revolver. He opened the chamber and laid the weapon on the table.

"Smith Wesson. 38. Police special, two-inch barrel. Five shot. It's been adapted for quick close quarter work. The handle has been re-balanced with rubber side grips, non-slip. The trigger pawls have been smoothed for a light action. The foresight has been removed, you just point, like a finger and, boom!. By the way, all numbers and makings have been filed off." He took out a box of shells and put in four. He looked at me.

"Leaving an empty chamber under the firing pin for safety", he said. Then he took out a separate chamber and put in five shells. "This is a speed-load chamber."

He demonstrated how the empty chamber could be slipped out and the new full one snapped in.

"You won't need an empty chamber for safety if you're firing, just enough to do a re-load," he explained. "Best place to wear it is tucked into your belt in the hollow of your back, But I'm also giving you a clip-on holster in case you prefer it. Try them out: see which feels best".

He sat down and looked at me thoughtfully.

"Where and when are you going to do the pick-up?" I told him.

"Yeah, that sounds reasonable. You've got great visibility there; no one could take you by surprise."

"Yes, well, I hope no one plans on taking me by surprise. Why would they want me anyway?"

I put away the pistol and we talked lightly about old times for a good hour. Then, ten minutes and three stiff whiskeys later I was on my way. We hadn't mentioned his broken romance at all. But we shook hands in a genuine commitment to keep in touch again now that we re-established. I said I'd come and stay and go to some horse race meetings so long as he promised insider tips. He wasn't wild about visiting London but he agreed he would come for a few days and stay with me. He was very enthusiastic about the theatre and I tempted him with the offer of getting West End tickets for a couple of plays he was very keen to see. Taking it easily over the uneven side roads I thought briefly about the gun. I was rather frightened by the thought of having it. It was still difficult to take the kidnap and violence seriously. But it was a pretty good shot – I had been with the battalion pistol club – so I knew how to use it.

As I drove back into Dublin it was late dusk and the lights were just coming on. I came along by the Phoenix Park where the racing would be then crossed the river. The Liffey looks particularly good at that time with reflections in the water from the neon advertising signs near O'Connell Street Bridge. After parking in the hotel garage I went to the desk for messages – there were none – and my key. Hotels feature hugely in the life of a motorsport professional.

Holly looked quite pleased to see me which was surprising

after our last meeting when she was virtually dismissed by a certain Irish lady. She was just coming into the foyer as I was walking towards the lifts.

"It's the Brit again. You following me around?" I walked round her slowly and gave a small appreciative nod.

"Yes, I've decided that I am."

In truth she looked very good. White trouser suit rather snug round the bum but elegant not tarty. "Pax and a quick drink." I said holding up my hands. Holly nodded.

"OK, Pax. We'll drink to the advantages of a classical education."

We went into the cocktail lounge this time, not the bar. A bit smoother.

"Bourbon on the rocks", Holly said to the barman as we made our way to a couple of chairs in the corner. He brought it, and my G &T. We touched glasses. "You, a friend of Gary Enders?" she asked without any warning. Her jet black eyes were free of guile - or so it seemed, but I remembered that she was an investigative journalist.

"No, thank you." I replied. "Definitely no friend of mine. I have to deal with him in a business connection. My job requires that. But we certainly aren't friends: he pinched my wife."

It just came out, like that. Holly appraised me thoughtfully.

"You know" she said. "I rather thought that you had been badly bruised by a woman at sometime. OK, you come on big time - in your face - but I'd say you are very wary about getting too deep emotionally."

What she said made me feel a bit feeble and ineffectual, certainly no lothário. But her look and tone of voice seemed to be sending me a different, much more acceptable message.

I shrugged and half-smiled back at her. She sipped her drink reflectively. Then she gave me such a long deep penetrating look - a real laser-scan. It seemed to last a long time.

"I think you are a regular guy", she told me at last. "I got some good vibes, when we first met on the French motorway; I dunno why, but I did."

With a quick flick of the wrist she downed her drink and I followed suit. Almost immediately she stood up, moving in such an interesting, feminine, way. She tilted her pretty head at a saucy angle.

"Come on, buddy-boy, I want to show you something which may interest you."

She led the way out of the bar and after collecting her key from the desk, went over to the lift. When it arrived at the third floor we got out and she marched purposefully down the corridor. I just followed wondering what she had to show me. I was thinking that it might be some documentary item relating to Gary Enders and his double-dealing. She was after all a journalist, and a pretty good one, I would guess. If it did concern Enders and that situation I should have to be careful. They still had Gabriella. But if she had some serious information I reckoned that it could be quite useful ammunition if needed.

Inside the large and impressive suite with its high ceiling and large windows she slipped off her blazer and threw it on a chair. Then she went over to a table by the window and took out an envelope which she brought over to me. The photograph which she showed to me was obviously taken by telephoto lens and somewhat blurred, but the features of the people were clear enough. They were Gary Enders and the Asian boss I had seen on the yacht in Monaco.

"Recognise anyone?", she was looking directly at me now. Brisk, business like.

"Yes", I said nodding slowly. "That's Gary Enders of

course. I don't know the other one; my guess is that he's one of Enders' contacts in the Far East. You know he's supposed to be negotiating some Grand Prix events out there – new territory for F One expansion in the new millennium".

I didn't know Holly very well. She was a journalist and this could be dangerous ground. She eyed me speculatively.

"Yep, on the face of it I'd say you could be right. But the odd thing is this was something of a secret meeting in a very out-of-the way place. Don't ask me how I know, or got the pics. And the other guy is a bit of a mystery man. He's not involved in trying to arrange race meetings; he doesn't own circuits. Word is he's a big wheel in the grey area of Asian business. Bit murky. I just thought maybe you should know that your pal Gary" - she winked – "is not mixing with the best people."

I said nothing and she took back the picture, replaced it in the envelope and walked over the table. She stuck the envelope back in the case and snapped it shut. Then she turned to me and said, " I'd like to show you something else." She unbuttoned her blouse with deft and delicate movements. Then she unhooked her bra and looked at me almost shyly as she slipped it off.

"Think you could be interested?" She came over to me almost cautiously. We stood close. Then in a succession of small movements, stopping to look at each other as if for reassurance we kissed. That first kiss was something special. Her lips had the taste of wild strawberries and of jasmine honey under her tongue – in biblical terminology. She stood back, pursing her lips as if making a big decision. Then she unzipped her trousers letting them fall to the carpet. She smiled at me before turning and walking over to the emperor sized four poster bed with its dramatic canopy.

All my senses were engaged now. She had the delightful high buttocks that many black athletes have. Superbly shaped legs from full rounded thighs to long slim calves. Not too thin. Just perfect. In soft silhouette against the light from the window she was divine - exuding a gentle sensuality. She dropped back onto the bed. It didn't take me too long to get out of my top clothes and I soon lay down on the bed beside her. She took one hand and put it flat against her right breast. Her huge eyes regarded me. When she spoke it was nervously

"Whaddya think of the old oojabongas?" I rubbed my palm lightly on the nipple with its fascinating texture.

"Very nice" I told her "the sweetest oojabongas I ever did

see".

Soon I was gently easing off her white satin knickers. Almost lazily she took out one leg and then the other. Now she was naked. I couldn't resist kissing her stomach, flat but with that rich female roundness as it curved down, it was the first time I had seen a black woman's sex and I was fascinated by the bright pink lips and opening. I was beguiled by the taste and by her scent. She threw me an Avanti condom from the bedside table. When I had opened it she rolled the condom on. It felt very nice the way she did it. Normally I take quite a long time but this was over fairly quickly for both of us. At the final moment she seemed so committed which pulled me in too. We lay for a few minutes afterwards. Side by side. Then she curled towards me and lay her head on my shoulder. It felt peaceful and perfect - as if I had come home. The sex had been terrific but the sense of pure joy was on another planet. I'd never, never felt it before. The big round white eyes with ebony pupils smiled up to me.

"Well, that was good fun, wasn't it? Mustn't get carried away though."

But she knew and I knew that it was much more that. You can't describe love; you can only feel it. I did. After a while she sat up. A beautiful breast pressed against my arm.

"You probably think I sleep with anybody who takes my fancy. I don't. Matter of fact I'm damned choosy. You probably thought I met you by surprise. Wrong. I'd been waiting for an opportunity. The rubbers by the bed were there for us. I kinda knew that we'd be doing it soon. But don't worry. No pressure. Don't feel trapped. But I'll tell you something. You ain't getting away from me, lover. This is something real special just like I knew it would be. Dunno why. But is. So it was great. No argument. But what I really like is the sensation in my mind. When you made love to me it seemed that our hearts were kissing."

I took her in my arms and kissed her hair, her neck, her mouth, her throat. We didn't say anymore just then, I got up and dressed.

I said quietly "Holly Bright, I love you. But I've got to go now. I have got some tricky stuff to sort out. I can't explain now but I shall later. I don't want to involve you at this stage. It's a bit... iffy. Do you know what that means"? She wrinkled her delightful nose.

"No. Well iffy means tricky, dubious". I paused. "It should soon be finished. Then I want to talk with you about the future

- us. It's definite that we are going to have a future - we both know that."

"Yep, I know", she said "and I understand."

I know I'm a dopey romantic but I have always used the words 'I love you' very circumspectly. Just strewing them around promiscuously would cheapen me as much as anyone. But this time I couldn't hold them back.

If anyone else had spoken the way I had I would have put him down as a pompous prick. But it didn't feel like that; no, it wasn't like that.

I began to sort out my clothes before dressing. Then I heard Holly's voice behind me.

"In the words of the old jazz song could you manage one moh time?". She was lying on one elbow giving one of her piquante lop sided grins.

I managed one more time.

Then I left her room sipping mentally a cocktail of emotions.. Passing through the lobby yet again I saw another fairly familiar female form – that of Kate O'Malley. She was as sleek and dramatically beautiful as ever. But now she didn't do anything for me. She hadn't seen me. I was glad, I cut round the other way to avoid her. Kiss-me-quick Kate was off my screen. Hell-o-o-o- Holly.

Chapter 12

There was a light mist swirling down from the mountains giving a rather mysterious, slightly sinister feel to the Lamb Doyle's car park when I drove in early next morning. I had come several minutes ahead of the meeting which had been set up by Gary Enders for me to pick-up Gabriella. I wanted to get the lie of the land. To check the routes in and out of the car park, to see where someone could hide. Of course, the other side would very possibly be playing the same game. There was an entrance at one end, an exit at the other. It was a vast area of parking for a relatively modest restaurant but it was a popular place for night-out Dubliners. The car - as I edged forward - seemed like an insect on a plate. I decided that I would wait right in the middle of the area, pointing towards the entrance, and keeping the engine running. The pistol resting in the hollow of my back was comforting but the last thing I had in mind was using it.

At five past eight on the Rolex, a black Mercedes saloon appeared at the entrance and paused. They spotted me quickly, although the mist seemed to be getting thicker. The Mercedes crept towards me and stopped twenty yards away. I didn't know what to expect. Nothing had been specified about the logistics for the hand over of Gabriella. I stayed in the MG awaiting developments. I was looking for some sign of Gabriella in the car but with the combination of mist and reflective dark glass windows I couldn't see a thing inside the Merc. The driver's door opened and an Asian wearing a chauffeur's uniform got out and walked towards me. I had a quick look around the parking area and then checked whether anyone else was getting out of the car in front of me. It seemed to be all clear. But I stayed in the car, and just rolled down the window. I had already the top down to give me a maximum visibility. When the driver got closed I looked at him and said,

"Where is Mrs Enders?"

When he spoke I recognised him. He was the guy who had accompanied me by helicopter when I went out to the Syndicate yacht at Monaco.

"You will please follow us and we shall take you to the place where you will find Mrs Enders. She is waiting for you now." I shook my head.

"That wasn't the arrangement. I was to pick her up now, here." He looked at me seriously and said in a rather anxious voice.

"I am sorry this was not properly explained to you sir. You see it would not be good to do it here: other people could come into the park - even the police. It must be done in a very discreet way. It is critically important for everyone. It is necessary, Sir".

"So why the hell was I told to come here? Why couldn't I have gone to the more discreet rendezvous straight away?"

He gave me a half-smile. Out of the corner of my eye I thought there might have been some movement in the Mercedes but I couldn't be sure.

"Please sir, I think you will understand that we have to be quite careful. It would not have been wise to meet you at the true rendezvous."

Of course I could see very clearly why they wanted to put a checkpoint in the hand-over plan. They didn't want a load of Garda Siochana crowding in on them.

"Sir, if you will follow us we can take you straight away to the place where Mrs Enders is waiting for you. It will only take half an hour."

"No deal" I told him, sounding like Phillip Marlowe. "Just tell me where to go and I'll make my way there."

"I'm sorry we can't do that. It isn't possible. The only way for you to obtain the release of Mrs Enders is to come with us, at once."

I did not like this one little bit. It smelled as fishy as Billingsgate. But I didn't seem to have much in the way of choice. There was no point in bluffing or threatening. Better to stay cool and keep some element of surprise -like the Smith Wessen. 38. I nodded briefly and before he could return to his car I blipped the MG's throttle and quickly drove up alongside the Merc. At close range I could see through the windows and I hated what I saw. Blondie, the Russian, a.k.a. Viktor. He didn't seem upset that I had seen him. In fact he looked rather pleased. His brief smile, more of an Ivan Skivinski Skivar sneer, spoke volumes. Then he looked away completely disregarding me, for the moment.

I followed the Mercedes out of the park as we accelerated away. He drove well, chauffeur style. Neat, fairly quick and keeping it all legal. Obviously he didn't want to be pulled in for a traffic offence. I thought that was interesting - were his diplomatic registration plates false?

The half-hour estimate was optimistic. As we climbed higher and higher into the Dublin mountains traffic became lighter and lighter. The turns and twists became sharper and more demanding. The precipitous drops were steeper....

We saw the odd car in both directions but there was no doubt that this was pretty desolate country. Turf, or peat bogs and wild gorseland. The only side roads were narrow tracks for the turf cutters' lorries. It was a soft day in Irish terminology the atmosphere heavy with moisture.

The mist now was almost fog and I was having to concentrate on keeping close to the lead car so that I didn't get lost. Headlights on and the high intensity lamps. Not having the top did help a bit.

Just after a tricky little bridge and up an incline we suddenly turned right, which surprised me. If I had been betting I would have backed left. This new one was still a narrow road but it was more than a track. We went down it for two or three hundred yards, then turned again, this time onto a drive. There were some dirty great iron gates but they were wide open and indeed they did not look as though they had been closed for many a long time. We went along the drive, fairly cautiously avoiding the worst of the pot-holes. Then, spectacularly out of the mist emerged an old castle. The sheer size and surprise were heart-lurching. It didn't quite have a moat and drawbridge but it had a hell of a big outer door encrusted with heavy black studs and protective bars. It gave the distinct impression of having been recently renovated. Now was the moment when I decided to take some control of the game. As the Merc drew up in front of the entrance I kept back, held some distance between us. The driver of the Merc got out and went to the huge door. Despite its medieval appearance it was obviously opened by a high-tech entry-phone system. He spoke into the phone intercom. The doors began to judder open on their elderly tracks and just as the Mercedes started to go through the gate I turned sharply and accelerated away back down the drive. I gave the impression that I was motoring hard to get away from the Castle, but in fact wasn't going far. I had noticed a small copse half way along the drive and I nipped into it, going well in, off the road. I stopped, jumped out and ran back to the entrance. There were no obvious signs that I had driven in but anyway I picked up a broken branch and swept across the entrance to obscure any tyre tracks. I also picked up an arm full of dead leaves from farther in and dumped them at the entrance. It looked quite convincing, I have to say. Obviously a misspent childhood playing cowboy and Indians had some merit. The last of the Mohicans lives on. Even so I decided to hedge my bets by leaving the car and finding a suitable hiding place. I avoided the open - although the thick fog blanketing the area was certainly a bonus. I worked my way round behind the castle. I wasn't sure what I was going to do but I intended to retain the initiative. They would still be thinking sequentially - probably reckoning that I had taken fright when I saw the castle and was going like the clappers back to Dublin for some help. I wondered what their response would be – would they send a car to pursue me? So far I hadn't heard a car going by.

I gambled that the last thing they were expecting was for me to make an entrance into the castle, uninvited, to see just what the set-up was. At least that's what I was persuading my cowardly inner-self to be the case. As I worked my way round I began looking for access points. It would not be the best of ideas to try to go in through the main door. I noticed that there appeared to be some wide culverts coming out beneath the castle and I dropped down into the hollow beside the wall, possibly a former moat, and had a closer look. The entrance to the culvert was a bit overgrown but I pulled aside the grass and foliage. It looked pretty wide and high. I took out the small waterproof torch which I always carry and flashed inside the passageway. It was dry and I clambered up and into it. I started out into the dark tunnel. I can't pretend I felt anything other than very scared and apprehensive. But pride, curiosity, a need to hide, God knows what – and damn and blast - concern for Gabriella - drove me into the unknown terrain. After perhaps twenty yards the passage started to climb and things became more difficult. As well as the incline the surface became smooth and slippery. If this was formerly a channel out of the castle for sewage and other unmentionables it obviously had to have a virtual path - down. And I was going up against the flow. This became more apparent as I had to look for handholds, ridges for my feet. Soon I was pulling myself up into a fairly narrow chimney. This was the worst scenario for me: I tend to have a fear of narrow, tight places. Probably I should admit to claustrophobia. I could never have been a pot-holer. Yet here I am working my way into a narrower and narrower tunnel which was also ascending at quite a steep angle. Claustrophobia how's your father? I was having to grit my teeth. I was sweating and it wasn't only the strenuous effort of pulling myself upwards. Suddenly the tunnel seemed to stop. I flashed the tiny torch beam onto the face of the stone work. I saw that the passage narrowed into not much more than a large bore drain. I felt terrible. Sick. Panic set in. I used some of my last resources of will power to control myself, to force a calm logical appraisal. I recited my mantra from a period of transcendental meditation. I got my breathing and my fear back under control .

The drain was wide enough to go through. Would it stay wide enough?. Logic said yes. Why should they make it narrower? Surely at the end where stuff was being sent down they would want it to be as wide and capacious as possible. Yes, well let's just hope the castle architect was a brainy and logical laddie.

There was only one way to find out. I squeezed my shoulders in and with the torch in my mouth I slithered and scraped my way forward. It was tight, very tight, too tight. I tried to breathe slowly and methodically. I pushed all thoughts of an itch at the back of my neck, well out of mind. Or tried to. My nerve-endings shrieked out when the drain tunnel made a sharp left bend. How could I get round?. It wasn't possible. But could I get back? I tried to push my body back along the drain but my clothes dragged. It was like pulling out a harpoon with the teeth going the other way to lock it in.. I felt real fear: blackness and a throbbing deep redness in my mind. I was hyperventilating - I could black-out. I could just get stuck forever and die here. I think it was that realisation which enabled me to steady myself. I attacked the corner in the drain. Inch by inch I got a shoulder through, turning almost onto my back in the way an experienced pot-holing friend had once described to me his difficult passage through an impassable tunnel. Just slowly, methodically. Stay calm. Once both shoulders were through I paused and then used the thrust of my legs to propel my body round the curve in the cave.

It was literally the turning point. The tunnel widened almost at once and became a channel much easier to move through. A sense of relief engulfed me. I paused for air, then scrabbled and clawed my way to the exit of the tunnel. I came out cautiously into a small chamber. The flagstone flooring was quite dry. I flashed my torch round the walls and suddenly realised that I was still incarcerated in a stone tomb unless I found a way out; or had the strength and nerve to return through the tunnel. Another stab of relief came when I saw the iron ladder, frail, bent and rusty though it was. I tracked it up it to what I hoped was an outlet. I wanted desperately to get on the ladder and get out of the dark, the restriction, the uncertainty. But I made myself think. I assumed that they would have been looking for me. There had to be a fifty-fifty chance that they had already found the car in the copse and would know that I was still in the grounds. They might just have discovered signs of my entering the culvert. I didn't know how many people were inside the castle. At least the two who came to collect me and somebody must have stayed to guard Gabriella - assuming she was in the castle. I could be up against a small army of well trained professional hit-men. Not nice. Why didn't I organised some back-up; Jonathan's private rugby team for example. Why hadn't I mobile phoned my whereabouts.

So what was my plan? What did I have in mind when I climbed up the tunnel? That is other than a totally irrational impulse. I now had a few basic aims: to get out of this chamber into daylight and fresh air. To avoid the opposition. Find Gabriella and get her out. And be very careful. I also quite fancied the idea of surviving in one piece, unmarked.

I took hold of the bottom rung, torch in mouth again, and climbed cautiously up. Another crucial moment. Lifting, opening. the lid. Would it open? Was it sealed-up by centuries of grime and dampness? Was someone waiting for me with a battle-axe? It moved at the first shove. I put my shoulder behind it and gradually slid it side-ways until there was a wide enough gap to put my head through. I moved up and slowly peered around. I was in the kitchen. The old kitchen. At least there was now daylight from some windows high up on the wall and I turned off the torch. The area showed no signs of habitation. The good news was that it obviously wasn't being used now to prepare food. The windows were dusty and not very large but after the tunnel it was like arc-lamp lighting.

I eased my body out as quietly as possible. When I stood up, my muscles tingled and spasm with cramps. I gave myself a few minutes to get back my balance and flex my arms and legs. Then I went to the kitchen entrance. I passed through a heavy door which fortunately didn't squeak. There was a door and I came out into a corridor. Everything was so quiet. A very narrow stone stairway appeared and I went up. My moccasins made no noise as I wound my way round its spirals. This time I came onto a larger wider corridor with a fibre matting running down the centre. I was getting near to the living quarters. As I turned the next corner there was a transformation. I was now on a balcony, carpeted and with wooden balustrades. Doors, presumably bedroom doors went off the balcony. There was a handsome polished staircase going down into the spacious entry hall. The bedroom doors were all unlocked. I opened each one with some care but I gave them only a cursory glance. I was sure Gabriella would be locked in. Half way down the staircase I heard her cry out. It stopped me in my tracks. Then she called out again.

"No", and there was a whimper.

Common sense went out of the window and I drew the pistol and raced down the stairs across the hall and burst into a drawing room from which the sounds had come. Gabriella was lying on a big solid oak table, hands tied behind her back. Her blouse and bra were on the floor and her upper half was naked. The Russian - Viktor - was standing beside her holding one breast and tormenting her nipple with a long bladed fighting knife. Gabby was twisting and turning to keep away from its razor sharp tip, crying out when it pricked the ultra sensitive areola. The blond Russian was smiling at her fear as she moved helplessly. He turned when he heard me charge in. At first his eyes narrowed when he saw the pistol in my hand; then he smiled again and moved the knife to the side of her throat.

"Drop the gun, Mr Piercy. Just one move and your lady will die."

The stupid thought went through my mind. 'No you are wrong; she is not my lady'. I pointed the pistol at him in the two handed grip which we were taught in the paratroops. I knew it was a hair-trigger. Could I hit him before he could stab the knife into her neck. He could see my indecision. "It's a Russian stand-off, Mr Piercy. Drop the gun. There's no need for it, anyway, we were going to let you take her away when I'd had a little fun."

I'll never know what I would have done next. I heard a tiny rustle behind me and then a sharp blow on my neck. I half turned to see the Asian chauffeur. He struck me again very fast knocking the gun away and then sending me onto my back with a swiftly delivered sidekick. It was all over in a flash. Viktor left Gabriella and he and the chauffeur quickly bound my hands with thick plastic tape. Then they pulled me up and pushed me into a chair, Viktor slapped my face drawing blood with his heavy silver death's-head ring.

He shook his head as if puzzled.

"I knew that you would come, my friend- if we made the

lady cry out. I guessed you were in the castle, you had to be. I still don't know how you got in, but here you are, and in very big trouble."

He walked back to Gabriella who was still lying on the table, and hitched himself up beside her. He sat, leaning forward, swinging his long legs easily.

"It's the end of the road for you. You were stupid to become involved. You are too far into it. We shall have to dispose of you. Pity about the lady, though; it is sad to waste such a wonderful body. But now you've both played your part and when the boss gets here he'll explain the little scenario he's arranged for you".

I was by now recovering from the karate blows and was feeling terrible; afraid, stupid, guilty. A bit of me was trying to think of something I could do. Nothing came to mind. Big Viktor looked at his watch.

"The boss will be here in about an hour", he said. "We'll have to think of a way of passing the time." He looked at Gabriella thoughtfully. She was still topless.

He paced up and down for several minutes. Then he signalled to the Asian who had been sitting quietly in the corner of the room. They spoke softly for a few minutes before the chauffeur nodded and left the room. He was replaced by a short stocky character who was definitely Russian in the good old Kruschev style. Viktor appeared to be giving him orders. I noticed the shoulder holster and heavy pistol. They both went to a side window and looked out. Then the other gunman went out and I guessed that Viktor had sent him on patrol or lookout. When the other man had left, Viktor went over the oaken sideboard and poured himself a large vodka. He tossed it back and poured another. He was a hard competent looking men, well dressed in designer jeans and expensive shirt. He looked again at Gabriella. He drank down the second vodka and moved over to her as though he was making a decision.

"Madame", he said "I have to have you. Before, I was only trying to get you to make a noise and get this man to show his hand, but seeing your body has excited me too much. I don't want to rape you and if you co-operate it will be much easier."

Gabby looked at him. In a sense this was something she understood. She shrugged.

"What can I do? she asked him. "I can't stop you. So you can do what you want, can't you?"

He ignored me at first, as he lifted her from the table and stood her against it. She looked light as a feather in his arms.

The large knife came out again but his time to cut off the sticky tape binding.

"OK" he said, "undress."

She unzipped her jeans and slid them down her legs with the knickers inside. Always a nifty un-dresser. She stood for a moment and any man would have had to appreciate the perfection of her body. It was the contrast of slim elegant limbs and soft rich curves which made it so special.

He made no attempt to kiss her mouth. Strong hands found her breasts, squeezing and kneading. But there was only one thing he really wanted. He turned her towards the table. She looked surprised but didn't resist. He undid his Gucci belt and opened his trousers. For the first time he turned to me as if he could see what I was thinking. And I knew very well what he was thinking. I also knew what he would soon be feeling. He played fair, I suppose. He moistened his fingers and carefully prepared her. Then he positioned himself behind her. I tried to look away but it was impossible. Once again I was seeing my wife, now my ex-wife, having sex with another man. I couldn't credit it. Viktor seemed frozen behind Gabriella, bent low down over the table, arms stretched ahead. Then her sudden gasp told me that he had penetrated her. I watched mesmerised as he thrust slowly into her. It was not long before he gave way to harder quicker movements and at his moment of crisis he was literally lifting her feet off the ground. I saw it all as though through a photographer's lens. He was then at his most vulnerable and I vaguely wondered whether there was some opportunity for Gabriella to exploit it. In reality there was no chance. He was still on her. His gun was in its holster; he kept it on while taking his sexual pleasure. When he came he looked like the cat who had the cream. I suppose he had. But he seemed a bit gentler towards her. He picked up the various items of her clothes and passed them to her. She turned away and began to dress.

"That was good, very good" he said in his deep voice, sounding very serious and nodding appreciatively. He turned sharply when Gabriella spoke quietly.

"Thank you", she said. "It was good for me too. I know that I am going to die and I just feel that in my last few hours I have experienced sex at its best."

Viktor looked uncertain, rather confused. But Gabriella was nothing if not a consummate actress and her demeanour, her body language was just right. She even had me wondering whether she was serious. But I knew her better. She was a clever girl and was trying to get some advantage from this new relationship, which had been forced on her. It was when she smiled at him, as she buttoned up her blouse, that she got through his defences. It was a shy loving smile. A smile of sweet sadness. He became apologetic.

"I'm sorry, very sorry. They will be here soon and I must tie you up again." He picked up the roll of tape and went over to her. She held out her hands, at the front which was clever. Then before he could start to bind her, she stood on tiptoe, placed her hands on his shoulders - just about reaching - and kissed him softly on his mouth. Then she put out her hands again. He stood still, for a long time looking at her. Then he taped her hands but not, I noticed, too tight. I thought that she might have had a shot at getting hold of his gun while she was kissing him. But in retrospect it would have been a stupid short-term move which would never have come off. She was playing a strategic game, keeping her nerve and that was much smarter

He led her quite gently to another chair near to me. He had lost his cockiness, his aggressive stance. Even tough men hard men have a chink in the body armour and I think Gabby had found it.

But... I knew we were in hellishly dangerous situation. I tried to calm my emotions, to try to think ice-cool as Gabriella was doing. I was beginning to do a mental check list of possibilities, opening my mind to the widest targets of opportunity, when I heard a car coming up to the house.

The big boss had arrived. Presumably he was the Asian whom I had met on the yacht at Monaco. I think I had annoyed him quite a lot but I'm sure he was not a man to bear a grudge. He just wouldn't think that way. He would simply eliminate me as a tiresome fly which was buzzing around; part of the process of completing his plans. Nothing personal, you understand.

There were sounds of voices outside, doors opening. Then Gary Enders came into the room.

Chapter *13*

If it was a thumping great shock when Gary came through the door, it was a double mule-kick in the stomach when Kate followed him a few seconds later. She was very much aware of the impact it would have. Looking taller and more striking than ever in lean-cut corduroys and a suede hipster blouse, she slowly drifted over towards me. She smiled but there was no humour in the eyes, just a diamond hand glitter, part smug satisfaction, part anticipation. She turned to Gary who had joined her.

"You know, love, I think this feller might have had a bit of an old surprise when we came in - would you say?" She leaned towards me and kissed me on the mouth.

"For old times' sake. It will be your last" she said.

I looked up at both of them. I really didn't have anything I could say. I just felt hopeless and helpless. I had scarcely got my mind back into gear, to start working out what the hell was happening, when Gary Enders spoke to me, almost conversationally.

"You always were a fool, Piercy. But you really are a bigger idiot than I took you for. You just walked right in - knight in rusty armour - to protect the delicate damsel in distress." He looked at Gabriella. "Some damsel; some distress." He shook his head, portraying disbelief.

"She was unfaithful, she dumped you for me, she was screwing me, your best friend, yet you still went right out on a limb for her. You risked your career, and now it's going to get you dead. You do realise, don't you, that we have to kill you?"

These were shattering numbing words, said so casually, in such a matter of fact way. And I knew, probably had always known, that he was perfectly capable of doing it. Just business, really.

"And I'm afraid the delectable Gabriella is going to go too." As she spoke Kate sounded quite intrigued with the idea. Gary was a ruthless pragmatist who could kill if necessary. Kate I could see, was a different animal, possibly a psychopath. I looked over at Gabby to see how she was taking it. Pretty well in fact. She wasn't going to let Kate get to her. I wish I had her guts. I knew damned well that I must look terrified, pale as a ghost and probably shivering.

"What is going on? What are you doing here alone? Where are the Asian Syndicate people?"

I finally managed to get the words out in rather pathetic, hoarse, voice. God, I must pull myself together.

Again, Enders looked at me dismissively. "There is no Asian super syndicate, no Asian bosses coming here. I'm the boss, the Asians work for me." He sighed pityingly. "You don't get it even now do you? I suppose at least I ought to put you out of your misery, not leave you wondering before you go."

He went and sat on the large sofa where Kate joined him. She was enjoying this.

"Quite simply I am going to take over a healthy slice of the world's auto industry and control it through television dominance using Formula One. Very much the plot I described to you in Estoril. But I am not the pawn being blackmailed by the Asian power masters. I've done deals with a number of companies, groups. I've got financial control of several. The big Asian car manufacturers will pay me nice juicy fees to set up the teams representing them, manipulate the system and provide the TV coverage to carry out their mass marketing programmes. In ten year's time there won't be any European motor industry.

But I needed a fall guy. When all the deals are done I can go to the official bodies and explain - the lily-white boy, how I discovered a plot by an Eastern group and have resolved it. You are, perhaps I should say were, behind it, working with a particular group - incidentally a main competitor in the car business to my consortium. The other competitor group is discredited and you, you can't argue because you are dead. I want you to know, Dan, that there's nothing personal in this, not really. You are just in the perfect role to deflect all the suspicions from me. Wrong place at the wrong time. But I must also tell you that I don't like you; I never have even when we were so called best mates. I think that's probably why I took extra pleasure from screwing Gabriella when she was still married to you." He turned to look at her. "And I can tell you that she liked it a lot."

What he was saying brought a tumult of emotions. Anger, inferiority, bitterness and fear; but mainly fear. Gary Enders continued his cautionary tale.

"You have always pissed me off. So damned nice, reasonable, not wanting to upset anyone. Well you bloody well upset me. Mr Popularity. All the nice stuff just came so easily to you. Well, I had to fight for it. OK, I'm a mean, tough bastard but I get the results - and I get the women. Most women. Most women prefer bastards." He grinned towards Kate. Then he looked over towards Gabriella. Her eyes were expressionless. This was one cool dame.

"And it was fascinating to see how Kate led you by the nose - or led you by something! We've been partners for a long time. She tracked every move you made. The only time she missed out was when you screwed up in the bar in Monaco."

This, of course, explained a lot. This was how they knew I had taken Gabriella to my cottage, how the so-called syndicate knew where we were, what I was doing. Kate had come to my apartment the night that Gabriella stayed. They had almost certainly been watching my house next morning and had followed us to the cottage in Oxfordshire.

"Of course" explained Gary. "We didn't want to be up-front doing the rough stuff. So we brought in our associates from Moscow, crudely and insensitively known as the Russian Mafia."

He flipped a hand in the direction of Viktor who had discreetly withdrawn into the background when Gary and Kate had come in. The other Russian must have been still outside in the hall presumably keeping watch.

"So you see how it's all going to work out." Gary spoke evenly. "You, and Gabriella were the schemers. She's been in cahoots with you - and in bed - for some time. We've set up a trail of meetings, messages - we've even got a recording of you both at it, that night in your apartment. The Russians are light - years ahead with bugging devices, long range microphones and, that high tech security stuff. You've also been observed, recorded, in secret meetings with mysterious Asians, exchanging documents. You see the story is, that I became very suspicious when you approached me in Estoril and wanted some information and senior contacts in the media world".

I could feel that he was warming to the satisfaction of telling this tale, making it microscope clear how astute he had been and how miserably obtuse I had been.

"The sad ending comes because you drive out here to meet Gabriella and pay off the Moscow boys. All the contracts have been signed and copies are in this case."

He held up the smart pigskin case which he had given to me before to hold the contract papers I was supposed have given to the syndicate representative. I noticed that he was wearing light chamois gloves. He saw my look.

"Yep" he said. "All the fingerprints on it are yours, likewise the papers." Then he smiled grimly.

"Unfortunately, when you arrive, Gabriella, who can't resist anything in trousers, especially if it's big, is having it off with Viktor here. You blow your top and batter her to death with this ancient Celtic battle-mace." He picked up a massive ugly weapon. He swung it gently in his hands. "I must tell you that this little scenario is all Kate's own work - she's very good at it."

I could see that Kate was looking excited and breathing rather quickly. God, how did I ever fancy this horrible, vicious woman?"

"Ah, well now that isn't quite the truth of it" she said. "I had a more interesting little play in mind, but Gary thought it would be better to keep it simple. And by the way", she turned to Gabby "I'll be wielding the mace when it comes to arranging your exit scene. You will go first of course, then we can get Danny boy's prints on the handle. I'll be wearing these." She dangled latex gloves.

"But look on the bright side: the good news is that you'll

have had a man - quite a man I'd say - just before you pop your clogs. What a way to go."

She smiled quite warmingly at Viktor. But somehow he didn't seem to be entering into the spirit of this programme. Of course, they didn't know that he had already taken Gabby not long before they had arrived. And I think it had left some sort of emotional residue. Certainly Gabby had encouraged that sentiment. A very clever move, although I couldn't see quite how it was going to benefit us. But anything could help. We certainly needed a good size miracle with a lot of bolt-on extras for good measure.

Gary hadn't quite finished telling us all about it, how cleverly it had been planned.

"So Dan, when you've killed Gabby in the violent anger of seeing her with him, just a couple of vicious wild blows it will seem, you start to take a swing at him. He's starkers of course, but he manages to get to his Ruger and fire, before you can get him with the mace." He paused mainly for effect, I'd say. "In fact, that is what he'll tell the Irish police by mail. After it's all over he'll disappear back to Moscow. The Irish police will be baffled when they finally come to the scene of the crime; it could be quite a while, this is a desolate spot. So Viktor will write to them from his totally safe haven in Moscow, deep in Mafia land. It'll help them to clear up the mystery, put away their file. They'll see the document case, and in due course they'll pass it on to the British police who'll contact the sport organisation body. Your scam will become public. I'll fill in the gaps, sorrowfully because an old friend had turned out to be such a crook and murderer. So everyone who is still living will live happily ever after. Nice one don't you think?"

I had been listening of course, but a lot of my mind had been desperately seeking, some ideas. There was a faint hope. I had to grit my teeth to speak at all. The bile in my mouth was acid and bitter.

"I think you've forgotten a few things. I told you that I had written down chapter and verse on this before I agreed to the meeting in Monaco. That's going to blow the gaff when it reaches the police. It will certainly put the spotlight on you and even if nobody can prove that what I've written is true, its got to raise big question marks."

Gary smiled and gently shook his head.

"Good try, old son, but it won't cut it. You should have been a bit more careful where you left the letter and notes. We removed them from your office safe shortly after you left for Dublin. Opening it was a piece of cake, the Mafia boys said. You could have left a copy somewhere else - but not at home, we've checked that. And we know that you didn't visit your lawyer because you've been under twenty four-hour surveillance. It did occur to us that you might have spoken with Jonathan - you had a long session at the hotel that night, so we were a bit concerned."

I cut in quickly.

"I didn't tell Jonathan anything, I didn't want him to be involved at all; we just spoke about his career: he's been receiving extravagant offers but I advised him to stick to Johnson Racing. So you don't have to worry about him: but I can promise you that there is a full set of incriminating material in a very safe bank vault". I realised that they didn't know about my meeting with Peter Sikorski.

"Indeed we don't need to worry about Jonathan" smiled Enders. By tomorrow night he'll also be dead. Very tragic accident when he's demonstrating the team car at the park. Stupid thing really - the whole car goes up in a ball of fire during the out-lap. Million to one electronics fault sparks fumes. The minute incendiary device is another one of the Russian gadgets; don't know what we would have done without them. Untraceable - disappears in the bang. Fired by radio signal. Really neat. And I'm sure you're bluffing about the bank vault. Too bad"

I didn't think I could feel much more grief than I was experiencing but this was a new sharp bitter twist in the gut. Jonathan was going to die because of me. If I hadn't involved him in the Monaco charade, he would never have been implicated.

"Look", Enders said briskly "we can't stand around all day chatting - things to do, lots to do." He called over to Viktor. "Have you got all the things we need?"

Viktor nodded briefly. He picked up a large bag from the corner and took out some light garments. He spread them out on the table. Enders explained.

"There's bound to be quite a lot of blood, you see, and these are slip-on coveralls which we can burn afterwards." Kate took one and stepped into it with her customary grace. She made it look like a fashion garment although I hardly appreciated it at the time. Gary pulled on his garment.

"Now, Kate, are you going to set the scene for Viktor to play his part?

Kate came forward and looked round he room. "I think

we'll have them doing it on the sofa. Let's take the bindings off: we don't want any marks or signs which the medical examiner may be worried about. Just keep them covered darling" she said to Gary.

Viktor took out the fighting knife from a hip sheath and sliced through the tape on my wrists. Then he did the same for Gabriella. For the first time I felt a flash of hope but Gary had taken out a Walther PPK with silencer - I recognised the Bond gun - and had us both easily targeted.

Kate was moving around like a film director.

"Now Gabby, time to get ready for it. Get your knickers off. I don't think Viktor will need too much encouragement but I expect he'll like to see the goods before he does his stuff."

For the first time Gabriella looked uncertain, stressed. She looked around, looked at me, looked at Viktor. She slipped off her blouse again, then the jeans. Standing in her underwear she was vulnerable and yet sexy. Kate nodded at her and she took off the undergarments.

"OK", said Kate. " Just lie back on the sofa."

Gabriella did it. It's a strange quirk of human nature that makes people go on doing things, obeying orders even though they know that they are about to be killed. Hoping until the very last second that something will save them. She lay back on the big cushions.

"Viktor, she's all yours" said Kate. "Do a good job now, dear man, it's the last ride she'll ever have. And we want a lot of forensic evidence, sperm. Signs of sexual activity, to keep the pathologist interested. DNA, all that stuff."

Viktor moved almost reluctantly to the sofa. He unbuckled his belt and pulled down his trousers. He climbed onto Gabby. We were all watching. It was horrific. Kate was obviously fascinated. When she saw Viktor's rather impressive equipment she looked over at me to assess my re-action. It would not have amazed me to find out that she had sampled it herself. After a few seconds his movements told us he was inside. I don't know how long it went on. Once again I was in a daze but I was somehow hoping desperately that it would help us. Could Kate in this sexual act gain some advantage? Time was ticking away. A cold icy thumb was squashing against my heart. It hurt. At the same time I could feel the perspiration pouring out of me. Cold sweat suddenly had meaning. Viktor finished with a burst of short movements. I think Gabby sighed gently. Kate looked as though she had reached orgasm herself. I just felt ghastly. Viktor pulled himself away and fastened his zip.

Kate moved to pick up the mace. She hefted it in her hands.

"Viktor" she said. "Put on the coverall. I want you to hold her while I hit her head."

It was unbelievably cool and yet for real. She smiled at Gabby. "I hope you enjoyed that Gabriella. It looked quite satisfying to me."

I thought I might throw a spanner in the works:

"Well, you should know", I said bravely. "I expect he has done you a few times."

She didn't like it. I could see that. Her eyes narrowed in a cliché.

"I think that will be quite enough of that sort of talk" she said. "When Viktor shoots you it can be quick in the head or in the belly maybe one in the balls for good luck. They say it takes a longish time."

Viktor was now in his coverall suit looking a bit like an astronaut. He took a step towards Gabriella then turned.

"She doesn't have to die", he said in his curiously high pitched voice. "I'll take to Moscow with me. She'll disappear for ever."

"Ah, no, Kate said angrily. "That won't do at all. She's part of the set-up. She's got to be part of the Piercy death scene."

"I can quickly think of a good alternative plot", said Viktor speaking slowly and forcefully. "We can arrange…" He got no further.

"No, no", said Kate. No way. She's going to die, now." My blood froze. This was it. God we were going to die - Jonathan was going to die... I didn't want to die.

Enders turned his attention towards Viktor. It was the only chance I'd have. Ever. I dived for the Smith Wessen which Viktor had kicked under the chair when they took it off me. I had been aware of it all the time. I worked out exactly where it was: which way the butt was pointing. I had repeatedly worked out the action. snap back the hammer. Pull the trigger. Don't attempt to aim, just point at the target, like pointing with a forefinger. What followed seemed to happen in slow motion but it was probably in milli-seconds. I reached the gun and snapped off a quick shot just as Kate was lunging at Gabriella with the mace. I missed. But Kate dropped the mace. She grabbed the Walther from Gary who was standing, almost jaw agape, not reacting. Kate, was very fast - ex IRA - and the first slot hit me in the shoulder, knocking my gun out of my hand, again. That gun and I were not destined to be partners. Then Kate turned very quickly to see Viktor reaching over for his big Ruger. I don't know whether he was planning to join in on our side to save Gabby; or to back up his original home team. We shall never know because Kate fired two slots into his heart from close range and he fell like a brittle broken stalactite. She had the situation more or less under control and she returned to me. I saw the flicker of indecision in her eyes. Should she finished me now, how would they re-do the scenario? Yes, I could feel her decide. Kill him now, then do Gabriella with the mace. The plot could still work. I'd often wondered what death would be like. She took aim.

"Kate", the soft Irish voice called out. "Drop it."

Liam stood inside under the window. I recognised the Browning automatic hanging loosely in his hand down the side of his leg. Now some other things became clear. Kate O'Malley was his ex IRA girlfriend. The great passionate love of his life. And she'd left him. Put him out to grass. Leaving him as a lonely tragic love-lorn figure. That's how he saw it anyway in his simple emotional way. It may sound Mills and Boone but real people do feel like that. Worried about the story I'd told him, he had decided that in addition to the gun I needed some additional insurance. So he'd followed me. Then he had seen Kate, and he had also seen what I hadn't - Kate and Gary together. He followed me up here and waited. He must have watched Kate and Gary arriving. He heard shots and moved in. So now he was standing there quietly telling Kate to drop her weapon. She turned towards him very slowly. Their eyes clicked-on. A stand-off. But not quite because just then the second Mafia man and the Oriental chauffeur both appeared through the doorway. Both were armed. Kate saw them and relaxed. She began to raise her weapon. As did her support team.

I wouldn't have believed that anyone could move like that. Liam was a blur of movement, like a formula one car passing really close by at two hundred miles an hour. Kate was quick but Liam was lightning. His first shot hit Kate, centre forehead, she was the most dangerous he obviously reckoned. Then the next two bullets hit the others, one immediately after the other, again, centre forehead. The three shots were so close together that it sounded like one explosion. Gary Enders simply turned and ran through the door. He jumped over the two bodies, sprinting it seemed for his life.

Now what? I thought. We're alive, thank God and that's

marvellous. But this is still a mess to sort out. And what about Gary? I took a snap decision. We had to keep tabs on him. I had to get him into custody before he could do any other damage. Then I had a sudden thought about the accident planned for Jonathan. I must get to the circuit to warn his team.

"Liam, a million thanks but you must get out of here fast. Clear all your tracks. Car tracks, everything. Then get out. Gabby, help Liam. When he is gone telephone the police, tell them everything - well almost- apart from Liam's role. Liam doesn't exist. Say somebody from the gang did the shooting. They fell out. Kate shot Viktor, the one who got away shot the others. Be vague about the description. Got it? I'm going after Gary. I've got to stop anything happening to Jonathan. I'll check with you later."

I rushed out of the castle entrance, then suddenly realised that I was bleeding. The shock still hadn't worn off. I looked at it. It didn't seem too bad, I think it was a nick rather than a bullet going right in. I hoped so.

I still had to get the MG. Enders was well away but I knew he had to go along the road we had used coming here. There was no other way. I took off running numbly down the drive, only the adrenalin keeping me going. The MG was still in the thicket and the key was in the steering lock. I was very quickly away and out onto the road. There were no diversionary roads and it was easy to follow the route back. The mist had eased which helped. I drove hard, pushing the revs up through the gears, virtually using a racing line through corners and banking on there being nothing coming in the other direction. Quick change third up to fifth skipping four. Heel, toe change down. Let it drift out a bit, bring on the power going out of the corner. Short change the gears coming up to the next hairpin.

As I reached the top of a fairly steep incline I looked down over the open peat moors stretching out below. I could see the narrow road ahead ribbon-like in light and shade. Then I saw him – dark silver grey Mercedes - leaving a train of dust about a half-mile ahead. I pressed the accelerator down an extra centimetre and the revs shot up. I'd have him soon.

Chapter *14*

I was definitely gaining on him. The big Mercedes 600 SLE was certainly not short on power but it would be a handful on the twisty narrow roads. The MGF had Formula One type suspension, double wishbones, and tremendous grip. It was perfect in these conditions. The numbing effect of the bullet hitting my upper arm was wearing off and it was giving me some gip, but the adrenalin was still pumping round the system and I don't think the pain was affecting my driving speed.

We were getting towards the end of the turf and gorse terrain and soon we would be on the proper tarmac road. But the route was downhill with the road falling sharply. There would be tricky camber and some high hedges; also the increased possibility of some traffic. A local farmer's car or even a tractor... That would not be good news. I reduced the risk of hitting oncoming traffic by cutting out wide going into the corner where I could see what was coming and chopping in tight. Anyway there were strong odds on the Merc hitting first anything coming the other way.

I don't know whether he knew that I was behind him and catching him and I wasn't too sure just what I would do when I caught him. But I still concentrated on doing it. On the next short straight I saw him just going out of sight round the bend at the end of it. Only two hundred yards between us. Surely he must have seen me? Now I started thinking what I would do when I got close enough. I could hardly force him off the road - a ton of Mercedes. The main thing was to follow him closely, not to let him get away. I moved closer and soon I was two or three cars length behind. I was driving more carefully now. I didn't want to be brake tested, if he suddenly stopped on the anchors to catch me out. He had been a useful racer in his day and knew a few tricks. It would not be great news to run up the bum of the battleship he was driving.

We came into the built up area in convoy, still tanking along still at about seventy-five. Inevitably as we came into the built up area we started to become involved in traffic lights, quite light at first, then building-up quite a bit. So we had to stop the racing. He was still pushing hard, seeking out the gaps which he could take advantage of, to get away. I had to stay on the qui vive, trying to anticipate his moves. I also had something up my sleeve: I knew Dublin better than he did. It had been a long time ago and there had been many changes - one-ways systems and, the usual changes in city road layout. But I had a feeling for the main directions.

Suddenly he dived into an inner lane and took a quick left. The road he had gone into was parallel to the canal and I knew roughly that it came out quite close to the centre near Rathgar. We went along as if on tow.

Some came signs up and he followed those going towards Phoenix Park. He was still driving much too fast, well above the speed limit and very aggressively. A police car shot over an intersection just as we came up to it. This must have made him think again about his speed. He certainly didn't want to be stopped for speeding. He slowed down and when we came into St. Stephen's Green we were moving at normal speed with the traffic. I was waiting for him to try something but eventually we turned right from Dame Street onto the quays. Past the Four Courts, Guinness brewery - a pint wouldn't come amiss - and then on the road along the park. It had become clear that he intended going into the circuit and I started to think about why. It suited me. I could get into Johnson Racing and warn them about the threat to Jonathan. Top priority that one. I glanced at the clock. Just gone five. The circuit would be open - in fact since it would be a free event there were no barriers to go through. But practise was due to start tomorrow and the teams would have their garages and motor homes set up. I could see the entrance coming up. We turned in into the very wide main avenue; its dimension always comes as a surprise. We went up a rather gentle long slope and he put his foot down to create a gap between us. Over the half mile or so to the circuit he opened up a bigger lead and he was probably two hundred yards ahead when we came to the gates into the trackside. I saw the motor homes lined up, plenty of space between them. O'Horan in Green and Yellow livery; Johnson Racing in its maroon and blue corporate colours. And a number of minor sponsors. Then quite a distance away was a large area, with its own marquee and motor home roped off. There was also TV equipment, a gantry and some other technical stuff. This was the site for Gary's operation. The nerve centre. I saw him hare off towards it. He left the car outside the ropes and dived inside. Even though it was a couple of hundred yards away I could see him unlock the door into the pastel silver motor home. He disappeared inside.

I pulled up at the Johnson Racing' site and jumped out. I burst into the motor home. None of the management team was there, I expected they would be in tomorrow. But Jonathan was there sitting sipping a coffee and chatting with his race engineer. I tried to speak too quickly, gabbled a bit.

"Jonathan, the thing I was telling you about has all blown-up suddenly. Gary Enders is a crook. He says that your car will be destroyed when you are in it tomorrow, practising. A fire bomb device or something". I looked at the engineer. "Check it out, carefully." Then I rushed out the words again to Jonathan.

" Gary is over at his motorhome. I suspect he's picking up papers, money and stuff. I'm going after him. Now."

I saw them both looking at me with some astonishment and concern. Then I realised that my arm and sleeve were covered in blood.

"Yep, I've been shot" I said. Jonathan came over to me.

"Dan, we must get you to a hospital, fast. Come on, forget Enders."

I shook my head and rushed out of the door; After a second Jonathan followed. The Merc was still outside the

Enders site. I went to get in the driver's seat of the MG but Jonathan beat me to it.

"I'll drive", he said.

We moved off with some wheel spin and just as we got away I saw that the Mercedes was also moving off onto the circuit. It moved off very quickly, accelerating hard and disappeared round the next bend, which was coming up two hundred metres further on. But where the hell was he going. How did he expect to get away?

It was Jonathan who gave me the answer. Out of the blue he called across to me.

"I expect he is trying to get to his plane."

Of course, there was a virtual airfield in the middle of the circuit and a few of the VIP's would have flown in using their private executive planes. They wouldn't be able to use jets - not enough runway but twin-engined props would be fine. I seemed to recall that Gary Enders had a Cessna twin. From Dublin he could fly anywhere in Europe, find a small, out of the way aerodrome and he could disappear until he got things sorted out. I was sure that he would have some runaway money stashed somewhere convenient and illegal.

We rounded the top bend and saw him going flat out down

the track. Jonathan took the MG up to 135 on the straight, nothing at all to him, and we began to reel him in. We drew even closer on the bends and corners. I could see Enders glancing backwards to see how close we were. It must have upset his concentration because the car jinked out of line and he had to correct quickly. Jonathan had driven an MGF before and was able to get the very best out of its agile handling. The airstrip came in sight about half-a-mile ahead. I was still trying to work out what Enders hoped to achieve by getting to the plane. It would take quite a while to get all the preliminaries sorted out and be airborne. We'd be on him very soon and he'd have no time to do much more than get inside the plane. But again I was a few laps behind in my thinking. I saw one of the planes start to taxi, and it was in Elder's corporate colour scheme. He must have telephoned from the car and asked them to get the plane ready for immediate take-off. The pilot would have had time to do the pre-checks and file a flight plan. So if Gary - quite often I slipped into using his first name in my thoughts - could get to the plane with a bit of a lead he could be in and away. Short of ramming the aircraft there would be little we could do to stop them just flying away.

But we were really close now and there was a possibility

of getting ahead and cutting him off. Good idea but again I was discounting Gary. As we got closer there was a sharp crack followed by a flash of light, then a hard metallic clang as the bullet hit the MG's bonnet. There must have been another gun in the Merc - fairly logical really.

It was another extraordinary scene. We were now out of sight of the pit area and the circuit was deserted. The evening was grey and dusk was settling in early. The clusters of trees - well back from the track - were quite still and the external presence was calm. Against this sylvan scene the crisp bark of the MG engine pushing well into the red on the revolution counter was a hard reminder of what this game was all about. And even more so, the bang of the gun being fired at us. OK: we were moving fast and he was firing from a wobbly platform - but we were too ruddy close for comfort and there was no guessing whether a stray shot might hit us or the petrol tank. In fact the third shot glanced off the edge of the screen - my side - and starred the glass. Two more shots seemed to go wide, then there was a sort of double explosion and the car slewed sideways. He had hit a front tyre and burst it just as we were coming up to the entrance to the airstrip. As the MGF shot sideways, I appreciated at Jonathan's skill. We must have been doing 130 mph. But he somehow let it dip down into a long slide and then to slow it down he flicked it into a double-spin scrubbing off speed and keeping the car honest. It all happened so quickly but to me it seemed slow motion and I can remember crouching well down in my seat, expecting us to roll at any minute. But we didn't, thanks to Jonathan's speed of reaction and delicate touch.

All this had tended to distract us somewhat from Gary Enders. But as we stopped spinning, amidst a cloud of dust and tyre-smoke, I looked to where I thought he should be. He now would have a pretty clear run with more than a fifty-fifty chance of getting away. For a start he could hop-over to France and disappear for a while in that huge country. There were small private airfields all over the place and although money may not be able to buy you love, it sure as hell could buy a lot of things. I had no doubt that he would have long term resources available to him though his allies, partners and paid acolytes. So it was going to be a long job to get him brought to justice, whatever that old fashioned concept might mean nowadays. Probably we'd never get him now. Realistically at least Gabby was safe and his plans for taking over - virtually destroying Formula One - were on the scrap heap. Thanks for the odd spot of good news I suppose.

It was a bit like a melodrama. The dastardly villain escapes at the end by the skin of his teeth and lives to play another villain in the sequel. All this garbage was burbling through my head as I saw him swerve into the entrance. There was a single post barrier across the entrance and it was down. Gary just drove the big Mercedes straight at it. A fraction before he put his hoof flat down to power the car through the barrier he turned to see where we were, what we were doing. It was instinctive I suppose. But it got him slightly off-line and instead of charging cleanly through the posts he caught one with the offside of the front-end. He was really motoring when he banged into the barrier rail and you could see that the impact with the side post made him momentarily lose control. He shot sideways through the gap and fought the car. He was an experienced ex-racing driver and I'm sure he would have regained control but at that moment a circuit maintenance van pulled out towards the gate. The driver was clearly unaware of what was happening - it all happened so fast. Gary had no alternative but to swing the bulky Merc sideways with a wild wrench of the wheel. This time he really lost is and as he managed to get it pointing forwards again I suddenly realised that he was going flat-out towards a small fuel tanker obviously used for refuelling the light aircraft. It was parked well to one side of the entrance on a concrete stand platform.

Gary must have driven head on into at more than sixty miles an hour. There was a terrific metallic din as metal was driven into metal, the splintering of glass and a deluge of fuel from the ruptured storage membrane. The grinding and mashing sounds went on for some time as bits fell off before the flying debris and dust seemed to settle down – almost in slow motion.

"Bloody hell", said Jonathan, goggle-eyed. "Bloody hell."

Then the whole shebang blew up. Highly volatile aviation fuel seeping, probably gushing, out onto the hot engine of the car would have fused the explosion. There was a smaller explosion as the car's front-end burst-into flame; then the brilliant orange fireball when the tanker went up, engulfing both vehicles completely.

We were a good hundred yards away but the heat blast was searing and there was some fallout; hot bits of metal were peppering the run-way; fortunately we seemed just out of range

"Bloody, bloody hell" said Jonathan again.

I couldn't say anything. A rather unpleasant thought did creep into my mind. This was really the best solution. That bastard who had brought the deaths of at least three people and was planning to kill Gabby and me without any compunction, probably deserved to die - to get his comeuppance. And a nasty bit of me felt glad. But it was a pretty horrific way to die and it also made me feel tacky to have this vengeful, rather vicious idea. Not the thing. I tried to ban such thoughts. By then we were both out of the MG and running towards the scene; maybe other people had been involved, perhaps we could help.

Gary Enders' plane had stopped back on the runway. Several people were also rushing towards the still burning wreckage. But someone who appeared to have a degree of authority was ushering them back. I could hear him calling out. "Keep back, keep well back. There could be another explosion. There's nothing to be done now. The fire-tender will be here in a couple of minutes. Has anyone been hurt by the explosion? Any first-aid needed?" He was right we could see that the remains of the car were glowing although it was difficult to identify much of it. There may have been a pool of fuel trapped and it could blow again.

The fire-tender swept up followed by two police cars and an ambulance. They drive round our MG abandoned on the track. I looked at Jonathan. And he nodded. He also touched my shoulder lightly.

"Better get this fixed, now." he said. He was subdued and badly shaken, I could see. Count me in for the same diagnosis. Slowly we walked towards the Garda cars. There didn't appear to be any senior officers - there hadn't been time. These were just patrol cars answering an emergency call: all credit to them they had got here very fast. There was a sergeant in one of the cars and I went over to him.

"Sergeant" I said slowly, "I can tell you a lot about this accident. But it's a long story. I want to get this arm fixed first. It's a bullet wound."

He looked at me sharply, his eyes crinkling interrogatively, under pale sandy eyebrows. A quick searching look at me, and at Jonathan.

"That'll be alright, sir," he said, "You get your arm fixed. Garda Walsh will go with you to the ambulance to see whether it needs hospital treatment. I'm telephoning the station and we'll have a Superintendent down here shortly." I nodded.

"Thanks. By the way, the MG out there is mine. You'll find

that there's a tyre burst by a bullet. A bullet also hit the screen, and I think you'll also find a hole in the front wing. But I can explain." He looked at me even more intently as if he was trying to decide whether I was a nutter or an IRA gunman. Then he looked at Jonathan and I could see that he recognised him: his picture had been in the Dublin papers for a couple of days, in features about top Formula One drivers visiting Dublin. The sergeant didn't comment.

"You'd better get that arm looked at, I'd say."

He called over Garda Walsh and we went down to the ambulance.

I was feeling pretty ropey. The gunshot wound, the tension, the chase were pretty frantic; and now the adrenalin had dried up I was feeling flat as a pancake.

I just about got onto the blanket on the ambulance bed before I conked out. They said later that I had lost a lot of blood and were very surprised that I had been able to keep going so long.

I vaguely remembered the ambulance driving-off, and that Jonathan was with me. That was it.

Chapter 15

It took quite a while to sort out the whole messy business. I was in hospital for several days and I missed the race meeting which went ahead despite the drama in Phoenix Park. The Press, of course, had picked up the news of Gary's crash and his death, but the police encouraged by the organisers, were playing it down as an accident. They emphasised the dangers of driving on a racing circuit in an ordinary car and the need for care in locating re-fuelling rigs. That sort of stuff. It didn't stay news very long.

The demonstration race was a huge success. They reckon that nearly fifty thousand people turned up. Naturally the O'Horan team got the special award. That's what everyone wanted: it was Frank's idea after all - and his home patch. Local boy comes good. The prospects of getting Dublin on the F1 programme were looking quite rosy.

I got to see the racing on television in between being interviewed by the Irish police. My British motorsport promotion went ahead, but I should have liked to be there to tweak the final pieces into place. Nonetheless, not at all bad publicity. Perhaps a bit less impact than I would have liked, but there you are. But in Dublin we didn't want to overdo the Union Flags ...

I still couldn't take in fully just how stupid I had been, how bloody naïve. Perhaps I was too close to it; and there was too much emotion. Perhaps I also wanted to believe that the mighty Gary, successful womaniser and multi-millionaire really did need my help. And I probably liked to play the Galahad rather than Lancelot. But it damned near killed me.

I told the police pretty well everything, just as I had asked Gabby to do when I took off in a hurry to chase Gary. That all seemed such a helluva long time ago now. I think they found the story of the shoot-out less than satisfactory, especially the unknown Russian Mafia gunman who disappeared after wiping out all the others. But they could see eventually that Gabby and I were victims not villains. We kept Liam out of it completely, I'm very pleased to say. He certainly saved my bacon and Gabby's. I had been worried about the pistol I had borrowed from Liam. It had my finger prints on it. But Liam had retrieved it and taken it with him. A very good move. They detained

Gabby for twenty-four hours, then released her but said they might have to recall her as a witness.

She came in to see me bringing a pile of sexy magazines.

"These will cheer you up" she said mischievously. We spoke a bit about the events being careful to avoid any reference to Liam. I wrote in the air "no Liam". She nodded. I tentatively referred to the sex incidents with Viktor.

"I've completely forgotten it", she said. "I've just expunged it from my mind". She squeezed her eyes tightly shut. It was so unusual to see her so intense. Obviously it had left some deep scars. "I just knew I had to do something - otherwise we would both have been goners. It was all I could think of. Anyway, it was what Kate O'Malley was planning to do to me afterwards that really got to me. Christ, she was a witch. You know, I think Viktor was intending to save me when he said he would take me to Moscow. Strange how things work out." She looked at me in slightly old-fashioned way. "Do you think you could arrange for me to meet that racing guy?" she asked, making the name Liam silently. She grinned to make the point.

"From what you tell me I think he" she smiled again, "and I, would have a lot in common. I mean, I don't think you are seriously interested in me, are you? You were a bit at first, I could feel that, but not anymore. Anyway, I know it wouldn't work really. What do the Italians say about sex relationships? Never drive the coach again along the same road when it's broken down once. A bit sad really but we are what we are. I'll tell you one thing though I don't feel sad at all about Gary. He can rot in hell for me. That was my biggest mistake getting involved with him."

I didn't mention the fact that even when financial restitution and outstanding debt payments had been made she would still be worth a small fortune with the money she inherited from Gary. Oddly enough he hadn't left a will and inevitably she was the beneficiary of his estate. I wrote down Liam's phone number for her and she put it carefully into the crocodile bag.

She came in a couple of times but on the last visit she met Holly who had come back to Dublin as soon as she heard that I was injured. Holly was sitting on the bed stroking my hand and whispering some beautifully wicked thoughts into my highly receptive ears. I was definitely on the mend and my self imposed description as a romantic sex maniac was fitting my mood perfectly.

Gabby came into the room and took in the scene in one quick glance.

"So this is Holly" she said. I had told her a bit about my new found friendship. "Hello, Holly." She walked over to us. I think I could judge her mood. She wasn't upset; she had no reason to be. Bu she had been married to me and psychologically thought she retained some possessive rights. However, she was a realistic and decided to give up any rights she might have, there and then.

"I don't know how well you know him, Holly", she said "but he's the best ex I've had. Mind you, my other ex was Gary, so not much competition. Dan is a nice, kind guy, not very practical and sometimes he irritated me like hell! But nothing wrong in bed. I want to see him in good hands - he can be a bit of a disaster when it comes to women. Don't mention the recently departed Kate." She sniffed in a most delicate feminine wrinkle of the perfectly formed nostril. She leaned over, gave me a kiss on the lips and said thoughtfully.

"I guess this is it, Dan. Get better soon and be happy. And thank you for saving me, even if not from a fate worse than death." Then she gave her hand to Holly.

"Goodbye, Holly. Look after him".

She dropped another pile of girlie magazines on the bedside table and walked decisively out of the room without glancing back. I wondered how she and Liam would make out.

I looked at Holly and she at me. Hers was a sweet confident look although she couldn't resist an impish note.

"I can see that your ex-wife still remembers your taste in literature." She said flicking the cover of Playboy.

There was a rich sense of intimacy between us now - ideas transferred automatically. She looked at me quizzically. I felt a hand slip under the bed covers. She found what she was looking for and established that it was in a suitable state. Indeed it felt as though it was striving to reach up to the moon. She got up and opened the door, clicking the engaged sign indicator in place before closing it and securing it with a chair under the handle. She took off her skirt and knickers before sliding into bed with me. As I felt her smooth thigh against me my nerve endings burst into flame. On this occasion she did all the work which suited me very well. After several days I was feeling very frustrated but physically still constrained by bandages and this was exactly what I needed. It didn't take long for either of us and she swiftly brought matters to a very satisfactory conclusion. I was left breathing hard.

I loved it when she said, "That was great, Limey. You

know I think I've got to find some way to keep my toy-boy very close to me, ready and available. I know a guy, actually my dad, who wants to start a Formula One Team to promote his company. He's president of the second biggest tobacco company in the U.S.. How about we go to talk to him, about you setting up a team and running it for him? He's got all the resources."

I lay back thinking. It wasn't a bad idea. Somehow I thought that my blissful job for the British Motorsport industry might be under the skids quite soon. I had been too closely involved with the Gary affair. Even though it was clear that I was in no way implicated there would be some stigma. And image is all in Formula One.

I had to make a report to the Council when I got back to London and the auspices were not good.

"Lets go and see your dad" I said, "I can also ask him for his daughter's hand in marriage."

Her jet black eyes gleamed.

Coming Soon the sequel to Chicane

"On Slicks"

"On Slicks"

Chapter 1

I was sitting morosely in my very spacious and comfortable hotel room in Atlanta. Everything had happened fast after Dublin. I resigned from my role as British motorsport ambassador. I think they were relieved to get me out of the way without any complications – or scandal. Holly and I saw her father and he was very receptive to the idea of my setting up a formula one team for him. We agreed pay terms – very generous by UK standards – and I began talking with his corporate publicity people and lawyers. They gave me a very nice office in the Tomahawk headquarters just outside Atlanta.

Holly and I were together a lot, both in the business and at home which was her swish apartment in Atlanta. She had a penthouse with incredible views over the city. At night the panorama glistered and sparkled. Helicopters like fire-flies seemed to be flitting round at the same height as the penthouse.

We got married quietly – by American standards – at her parents' house. A 'Dallas' kind of affair by the pool but much classier.

But now only six months later we were in trouble. A few silly rows at first. Then some anger. We both realised that we had to try harder and did. The sex was still wonderful but the loving 'feeling', on her part, seemed to be slipping away.

So what the hell is wrong with me? Just how could it have gone so wrong? Why wasn't working out with Holly? I still can't believe it. We were so much in love. Or seemed to be and I think we still are. I'd never felt like that before. Well, maybe with Gabby at the beginning. When she left me for Gary Enders I thought I would never feel that joy again.

Loving someone so that they were the most important thing in the world - more important than life. How can it change, so much? It just does. First I'd lost Gabriella, now Holly. It had to be something in me. Losing one wife is unfortunate; losing two is extremely careless, to parody Oscar Wilde.

Anyway it looked as if I'd blown it and now I was in a pickle. I had set up the Tomahawk GP Team for Holly's dad with its corporate headquarters close to Boston. The manufacturing base was in the UK - on the outskirts of Reading. Pretty handy for Heathrow, Silverstone and a lot of engineering specialists and carbon fibre fabricators. Everything had been shaping up well; I'd managed to bring in a top designer and experienced engineers and a leading driver had pencilled a provisional agreement. I also had a very interesting development in hand: the first black driver in Formula One. A very talented young man I was looking forward to managing. This could now be a complication because he is a second cousin of Holly.

We were ready to go next season. I had managed - with the help of Bob Bright to get a very good engine deal with a major US manufacturer. They quite liked the idea of working with an American team - even if its technology was British based. It met some commercial image building objectives in both countries.

Holly's father was a pretty big wheel in US business world and Tomahawk Tobacco with its uniquely low tar rating, was one of the new cigarette brands, especially popular among the younger set who liked the style of smoking but were not keen on lung cancer. I got on well with him. He had given me a lot of freedom and a lot of dollars to get the team in place. I thought that he would wish to go on with it. It was after all a well thought through business arrangement. And he was worldly – wise and knew that marriages sadly could just break down.

The young black driver was a distant relative and had come to me via Tomahawk. I wanted to see the project though, to start a successful team.

But I also wanted Holly. I picked up the telephone and called her number. She didn't do any of her jokey stuff. She just said

"I'm really glad you called, Dan. Can you come over?"

Chapter 2

At the speed I was travelling I think I was lucky not have been picked up by the Highway Patrol. The Americans are totally dedicated to the automobile, their lives and cities are built around them, but their speed limits are notoriously low and rigorously enforced. This time I escaped the black sunglasses stare and "HI, Mr Stirling Moss". Strangely Stirling Moss is the still the remembered British speed man.

As I was pushing the Jaguar XKR into the mauve hued sunset my mind was racing equally fast. What did Holy want? Was it good or bad news? Did she want a divorce - or possibly a reconciliation? Put my name down for the latter option - please. I drew up into the expansive parking bay in front of her apartment. For a couple of minutes I sat gathering my thoughts and getting my emotions under control. I got out, carefully blipped the electro-car key and stepped into the elegant foyer.

The smart hall porter in his freshly pressed khaki suit knew me.

"Good evening Mr.Piercy. Miss Holly is expecting you.

She said to go right up. I'll buzz her to let her know you are on your way".

The lift opened into the apartment and she was waiting for me wearing a simple, though doubtless expensive, gun-metal trouser suit. I knew from her look that everything would be fine. I stood like a ninny at the entrance just looking at her. Then we both moved forward simultaneously, collided and she was in my arms. I just held her and she held me right back. We walked over hand in hand to the large panoramic window and sat side by side looking out at the embers of the sunset.

"I've been so unhappy" she said quietly. "And I think I've been very foolish. Looking back I think I just hadn't got used to the idea of being married - being part of another person's life. I think you can guess that I've been pretty much spoiled and at the same time very independent. But I'm absolutely sure that being with you, living with you, sharing a life with you is what I want. I hope you still want me".

My feelings welled over , I could almost taste the tears. I kissed her gently.

"Heh" I whispered close to her ear. "I've been kicking myself all around those lonely hotel rooms for being such an idiot. I love you and I'm so happy to be back with you".

She sighed softly and I kissed her again. She put her arms around my neck and things began to develop inexorably. Then the phone rang. It was on the answer-phone and Holly waited to hear who was calling before breaking our clinch.

"Holly. This is your Dad" cam the voice. "Can you pick up if you're there, its kind of important sweetheart". Holly looked at me wryly. I smiled and shrugged and she went to the phone.

"Hi Dad, what's the problem?" She asked and listened for a few minutes and then spoke again.

"OK Dad. Sounds weird. Dan's here now and we'll both come into the office tomorrow morning". She raised an eyebrow and I nodded.

"All right Dad. See you then…. And take care. I guess Jimmy is around? Good. Bye".

She came back to the sofa and slid beside me.

"Dad's been getting some threats - not exactly sure what about but it seems it might concern the team. He was worried about me. I said we'd both see him tomorrow. In the meantime I think you'd better stay right her tonight to look after me"

Sounded good to me.